When the Streets Clap Back 3

Lock Down Publications and Ca$h
Presents

When the Streets Clap Back 3

A Novel by *Jibril Williams*

Lock Down Publications
P.O. Box 870494
Mesquite, Tx 75187

First Edition August 2018
Printed in the United States of America

Lock Down Publications
Like our page on Facebook: Lock Down Publications @
www.facebook.com/lockdownpublications.ldp
Cover design and layout by: **Dynasty Cover Me**
Book interior design by: **Shawn Walker**
Editor: **Tisha Andrews**

Stay Connected with Us!

Text **LOCKDOWN** to 22828 to stay up-to-date with new releases, sneak peaks, contests and more…

Thank you!

Submission Guideline.

Submit the first three chapters of your completed manuscript to ldpsubmissions@gmail.com, subject line: Your book's title. The manuscript must be in a .doc file and sent as an attachment. Document should be in Times New Roman, double spaced and in size 12 font. Also, provide your synopsis and full contact information. If sending multiple submissions, they must each be in a separate email.

Have a story but no way to send it electronically? You can still submit to LDP/Ca$h Presents. Send in the first three chapters, written or typed, of your completed manuscript to:

LDP: Submissions Dept
Po Box 870494
Mesquite, Tx 75187

DO NOT send original manuscript. Must be a duplicate.

Provide your synopsis and a cover letter containing your full contact information.

Thanks for considering LDP and Ca$h Presents.

Chapter 1

"What the fuck! Where the fuck you get the chain from?" 40 snapped, grabbing ahold of the chain and Vanessa.

"Just calm down, Rob. This is my brother's chain." Vanessa thought 40 was mad because he thought she was rocking another nigga's jewelry.

"Bitch! This ain't your brother's chain! This shit belongs to my nigga Block! Who's the fuck—"

Boom! Boom! Boom! Boom! Boom! Boom!

40 jolted up in bed abruptly from his nightmare. The excruciating pain exploded in his jaw and his left shoulder, forcing him to fall back onto the bed. The pain in his jaw was so intense it felt as if he was slapped with a Louisville slugger. The pain seemed to make the room spin. 40's body broke out in sweat. He tried to call for help but for some reason, he couldn't move his mouth. His tongue felt dry ass sandpaper. He grabbed ahold of the railing on the bed as he tried to steady himself. He breathed deeply in and out of his nose

The pain was still there, but he was slowly gaining his bearings. He fought hard to focus. He reached for his throbbing shoulder only to find it was covered from his shoulder to wrist by a cast. Reaching for his face, he found it swollen and tender to the touch. The left side was covered in bandages. Noticing an I.V. lodged in his right arm, he followed the clear tube to the I.V. pouch.

Taking in more of his surroundings, 40 took note of the 24-inch T.V. that occupied the right corner of the room. Seeing himself in a gown, 40 knew he was in the hospital, but he didn't know what had transpired for him to be there. An elderly, chunky nurse entered the room.

"I see that someone has awakened. I'm Nurse Gibblings. I'll go get your doctor once I check your vitals and change your bandages." Nurse Gibblings had that grandmotherly feel about her, the kind that no matter who you were, she'd always have the remedy to fix all of your problems. "You had me worried, young man. I prayed over you all night asking God to bring you out of this bad situation," she told him, checking the monitor that stood next to 40's bed. "You came in here all shot up, blood was just everywhere," she said, shaking her head as she mentally encountered the events that took place just three days ago. Nurse Gibblings caught the baffled look in 40's eyes. The monitor beeped loudly indicating that his heart rate was elevating at a rapid pace. "Calm down, Mr. Pulley," Nurse Gibblings said, placing a motherly hand on 40's good arm. The dam of memories broke and the recollection as to why he was in the hospital came flooding back, hitting him like a typhoon. 40 tried to speak as he fought through the pain.

"Va—Vanessa," 40 whispered through clenched teeth. Nurse Gibblings couldn't make out what was being said.

"Listen, baby. You're gonna have to take it easy. You've been shot in the face. The bullet fragment broke your jaw in two different places. I'm going to go get your doctor so he could explain everything to you," she told him, exiting the room.

"No!" 40 grappled to get her attention, but his plea fell on death ears. 40 laid there realizing the dream he was having earlier was nothing other than a living nightmare. He remembered arguing with Vanessa about wearing a chain that belonged to his deceased friend Block before shots rang out. *"Where's Vanessa?"* he thought to himself. The palms of his hands became moist and his heart rate once again became rapid, panic starting set in. *"What had happened to her and the baby?"* 40 thought. Just the notion of losing anyone of them made his eyes glaze over with tears threatening to fall. A tall, Caucasian man came into room followed by Nurse Gibblings.

"Good afternoon, Mr. Pulley. I see that you are awake and alert, and that's a good sign. I'm Dr. Edelman. Let me explain your condition to you. You were shot three times. One bullet struck your humerus bone, which broke the bone in between your elbow and shoulder," Dr. Edelman said, pointing at the cast that held 40's arm. "Another bullet was lodged in the bottom of your left foot. We removed the bullet, but you will walk with a slight limp for the rest of your life. You also were shot in the face. Well, the bullet must have ricocheted off something and struck you in the jaw, breaking it in two different places. God was with you, Mr. Pulley. You might not have been lucky if the bullet would have gone three inches up and hit you in the brain. We removed the bullet fragment from your jaw, but there is a very small piece located in your tongue." Dr. Edelman paused to see if 40 comprehended what was being conveyed to him.

40 moved his tongue around in his mouth. He barely could due to all of the swelling, but he wasn't concerned with the condition he was in now. He knew the was alive and being alive was a sure sign to him that he had overcame the worse part of his situation. His mind and heart was on Vanessa and his unborn child. He had to find out about Vanessa.

"Va—Vanes—sa," 40 struggled through the pain to pronounce her name.

"Please don't try talking," Dr. Edelman advised him, walking closer to 40's bed, but he was persistent.

"Va—Vaness—sa!" he forced out though his wired shut jaws. The pain he was experiencing brought tears to his eyes, spilling over and leaving a trail of wetness down his cheeks.

"Mr. Pulley what are you trying to say?" Nurse Gibblings asked, walking over and placing her ear close to 40's lips. He took in a deep breath through his nose and exhaled just as deeply, trying to will himself enough strength to speak.

"Vanessa, my—my girlfriend. The b—baby." 40 let out a deep breath, his chest rising and falling with great effort as he waited impatiently for his words to register to Nurse Gibblings.

She repeated what he said to herself. "Vanessa, my girlfriend. The baby." What he said had now become clear to her, realization making her drop her head in a remorseful kind of way.

40 didn't miss this gesture.

"Errrrrrh!" 40 made an unnatural sound while he stared Nurse Gibblings down, trying to force her to tell him what she knew about Vanessa.

"I think it's best that Dr. Edelman to tell you what going on with your girlfriend, Vanessa Jones," she said, eyeing Dr. Edelman.

"Well," Dr. Edelman said, holding a medical chart in his left hand and feverously clicking a ballpoint in the other. " Ms. Vanessa Jones is in grave condition. She sustained a gunshot wounds to the neck and chest which ultimately caused her to lose a lot of blood. Ms. Jones is recovering on the second floor in our I.C.U. unit. She is not out of harm's way yet, but she is young and that's working in her favor. And as far as the baby goes…" Dr. Edelman paused, not sure if he wanted to pass the next bit of information on to 40, but he continued. "We're not expecting the baby to live. This situation has placed a great deal of stress on the baby. If the baby does survive, we don't know if there will be any physical or mental damages as a result of this," he stated with firmness in his voice.

40 pondered the doctor's words. He made up his mind that he needed to see Vanessa. He needed to be near her and his unborn child. Throwing the covers back from off his body, 40 swung his feet to the floor in one swift motion.

"Hold up, Mr. Pulley. You are not in any condition to be going anywhere right now," Nurse Gibblings pleaded with him, placing her hands on his shoulders as she tried to keep him seated on the bed.

"Errrrrrh!" 40 let out another beastly noise before he took a swing at her, knocking her to the floor. He had to get to Vanessa by any means. He had his mind made up that nothing was going to stop him. 40 stood to his feet but only to crash to the floor, falling next to Nurse Gibblings. The pain that erupted from the bottom of his foot was paralyzing. Dr. Edelman snapped out of his state of shock, rushing over to them. 40 hollered and kicked with his good foot at him, trying to defend himself as he became hysterical.

Dr. Edelman called for assistance, flooding the room with nurses and other doctors who held him down. Dr. Edelman then took a syringe out of his white lab coat, inserting it into 40's arm. The dose of Demerol instantly relaxed him. His body went limp, but his mind, heart, and soul cried out for Vanessa and his unborn child.

Chapter 2

"Here, baby. Take this." Tashia handed BJ some Morton 800 with a glass of orange juice and a turkey, egg and cheese sandwich.

"Good looking," he said, throwing the pain pills in his mouth and chasing it down with the orange juice. BJ devoured the sandwich in six bites.

As he watched ESPN on his 70-inch, Sony television, Tashia sat next to BJ on the couch. She then picked up the bulletproof vest that rested on the coffee table that sat in front of her. She traced her manicured finger over the bullet impressions that were placed in the vest three days ago. She did every chance she'd gotten. She was amazed as well as traumatized. She was amazed at how this thin material could stop a bullet, let alone stop two of them. She was also traumatized because BJ had on this same vest, which meant someone had tried to kill her man.

She was thinking that 40 made the attempt on BJ's life and that didn't sit too well with her. However, thanks to the bulletproof vest, he was sitting next to her with a set of bruised ribs.

"Baby, we need to talk," Tashia told him, grabbing the remote and turning the volume down on the television a few notches. BJ looked at the love of his life and saw the seriousness in her eyes. He gave her his undivided attention, hoping she wasn't going to go into the bag of twenty-one questions about the night her came home with his ribs bruised and a shot-up vest.

"What's good, Tashia?"

"He knows," she said in a low voice.

"Who knows what?" he asked, looking confused.

"40 knows that you killed Skalez," Tashia blurted out.

"How the fuck he knows that?" BJ eyed her with suspicion. The only person that knew about him killing Skalez was Tashia and Homicide Jack. She only found that out by default, ear hustling when he confided in Homicide Jack's about Skalez's murder. That raised his antenna since he knew she was aware Skalez and 40 ran in the same circle.

"Three days ago, I got a call from 40. He told me he found out your boy Lil Chris was the person that Skalez bodied the night you two ran up in his house." She paused to see if he was following where she was going before she continued. "40, putting two and two together, figured out that you and Lil Chris was crime partners. So, he's thinking if Lil Chris was killed by Skalez, then you were there to kill Skalez, making a getaway with the money. He's really convinced you're Skalez's killer since you knew about the money from the caper they pulled on Lance," she told him, looking at her lover with concern.

BJ couldn't believe the shit storm his life just rained down on him. He let out a sigh of pure frustration. The anger in him started to boil. *Shit. 40, since you got beef, I got the heat to cook it,* BJ thought to himself. BJ was thankful he was already a step ahead of the game. He already commissioned a contract on 40's life, but he had one problem though. He had paid Homicide Jack $50,000 to handle the hit, but nothing had happened as of yet. Homicide Jack was laid up in Riverside Hospital with a bullet in his shoulder and hip. "So, he called you three days ago?" BJ asked her.

"Yeah, the same night you came home wearing this thang all shot up with cracked ribs," she told him, still holding the bullet proof vest. BJ studied her body language.

"So, what made you wait so long to tell me? You know he put them slugs in that vest that you're holding?" BJ lied with a straight face. Tashia instantly got defensive, frowning her face up.

"BJ, I know damn well you're not sitting there insinuating I knew about this and didn't try to warn you. I called you as soon as I got that call from 40 about you, but you didn't answer your phone." BJ just stared at her with that dead man stare. He knew she was telling the truth because Toflon was the nigga who tried to kill him three days ago. Still, he had an angle to play. "Look, BJ. In the past, 40 and me did business together.

I baited niggas in and him, Skalez and Block would rob them all. But my loyalty lies with you. I can promise you that," she said with tears in her eyes. "I didn't have to tell you I heard you telling Homicide Jack that you killed Skalez. I could have taken that information straight to 40 but I didn't because I love you, BJ," she said with tears running down her cheeks. She was being straight up with him, but he had to play his trump card.

"I believe you, Tashia. Sorry for taking you through that. You know that a nigga be in them streets and all type of switch ups and double crosses be coming at me. I just needed reassurance that you're with me one hundred percent," he stated, taking a deep sigh as he wiped tears from his lover's face. "I need to ask you something though?" BJ paused. "Naw, I can't ask you no shit like that," he said, shaking his head.

"What is it, baby?" she asked. She was willing to do anything for her soon-to-be hubby to prove she was all for him. BJ took a minute to ponder on his thoughts.

"Set the nigga up for me. Let's end this shit so we can get married and have us some little shorties running around here with the two you already got. Let's live life, baby." Tashia didn't even hesitate or think twice about what he had just asked her to do.

"Let's go, boo," she agreed, looking into his eyes without breaking eye contact.

She wanted him to see the sincerity in her eyes. BJ nodded his head up and down in agreement. He respected Tashia's gangsta. He leaned over and grabbed the back of her head, pulling her in for a kiss. Passionately, their tongues touched and made love in the own way. BJ sucked on her bottom lip. Her nipples grew hard as a Jolly Rancher through her wife beater. Her love juices saturated the crotch of the gray thongs she wore. She pushed them to the side, her love box making a gushy sound as she inserted two fingers inside of her woman cave. She continued to kiss her lover with great vehement as she worked her fingers in and out of her love box.

"Don't you want to taste me?" she whispered in between their lip lock.

"Mmmmhmm," he replied.

She withdrew her dripping wet fingers from between her legs. Her fingers were wet as she placed them in his mouth. He savagely sucked them dry, his manhood growing stiffer as he fought to be freed from his jeans.

"Damn, baby. Your pussy taste so fuckin' good," he said, grabbing his hardness. Tashia took ownership of his hardness, stroking him through his jeans. BJ went back in for another kiss. She removed his member, watching it stand straight up like a soldier called to attention. She grabbed him and stroked him softly, admiring the texture of his fatness.

She loved BJ without limitations, the connection they had was something she had never experienced with a man before. She loved the fact he didn't act macho around her or tried to control her every existence like most men had a tendency to do. The night he asked her to marry him, she knew at the moment she would be the best wife she could be for him, even if it meant she had to slide back into her grimy ways.

Tashia used the precum that oozed out the head of his manhood as lubrication to skate up and down his full eight inches. BJ winced from the pain in his rib area. He lifted up to slide his jeans over his hip, giving Tashia full access to him. She positioned herself between his legs, French kissing his member with its bell pepper shaped head.

BJ eased his hand down her wife beater. He pinched and pulled on Tashia's nipples, making her breath get caught up in her throat. She deep throated him to the base, holding him there as she worked her head in a circular motion. The skill she was putting down on him came from watching the porn star Cherokee in her highly sought out porn movies.

"Fuck, baby!" he blurted out.

She came off BJ's manhood, letting a popping sound escape her mouth like she would if she pulled a blow pop out of her mouth. *Pop!*

"Am I hurting you, baby?" she asked with concern in her voice. She knew his ribs were tender, not wanting to do anything that could cause him any discomfort.

"Naw, Tashia. Do you, ma," he replied.

She inserted the meaty part back into her mouth and caught a slow up and down rhythm on him. It didn't take long before BJ exploded in her mouth. She continued to outdo her own major head game. It was so good. It had him with his ankles turned inwards. She went down to the base of his shaft, wrapping her lips tightly around him. She slowly came back up, bringing the last of his juices up with her.

BJ's head fell back on the leather couch cushion. He exhaled, letting the feeling slowly creep back into his ankles and toes.

"You ok, daddy?" she asked softly and seductively, but he couldn't deliver any words. All he could do was move his head up and down.

She went to the bathroom to get a wet washcloth to clean him up. She did it with such care, passing him an Atimo full of Kush at the same time. He contemplated his next move, knowing he had to murk 40 the first chance he got.

The only advantage he had over the situation was 40 being aware that he knew he wanted him dead. BJ knew he had to heal up and get ready for war. He wasn't sure if he would have to set 40 up or not. He loved Tashia too much to put her in harm's way, but it wasn't something he could easily just throw to the side either.

His mind drifted to Toflon's bitch ass. He almost ended BJ's young hustling career. BJ rubbed both spots on his abdomen where the bullets struck the vest. He picked it up and laid it next to him, copying the same motion he'd seen Tashia do earlier. He traced the impression where the slugs struck. He shook his head and whispered, "Thank God for Kayaker."

Chapter 3

Moe-B coursed through 24th street to check the trap out. He wanted to see the aftermath of the shootout. He had strict orders from BJ to stay away from the block but at the moment, he was moving on his own accord. The crime scene tape was lying on the ground in front of it. The entire block was a ghost town. There wasn't a smoker, cat, or mangy dog in sight.

Moe-B stopped his all white Charger sitting on black rims in the middle of the street right in front of the bullet-ridden trap house. This is where him and his cousin Lil Tate sold work for BJ and his uncle Homicide Jack.

His mind slipped back to the night he killed his own flesh and blood, seeing the white chalk sketched on the ground where his cousin Lil Tate took his last breath.

The nigga with the Mack was standing over BJ, ready to air him out. Moe-B had to do something. He could see through the van where he was waiting. He put it into gear and pressed hard on the accelerator, making the van jump the curb. He headed straight towards the gunman that was still standing over BJ. Moe-B gritted his teeth and braced himself on the steering wheel ready for impact. The gunman saw him coming. He dove out of the way before the van could strike him, causing him to crash into the side of the trap house. The gunman got up from the ground and ran into the alley, barely escaping with his life. Moe-B jumped out of the van and sprinted to his uncle's side.

"Unc, you alright?" Moe-B asked him.

"I'm hit, nephew. Get me in the van," Homicide Jack said in pain. Moe-B got out to help him. He could still see BJ moving on the ground. Once he helped his uncle in the truck, he yelled out, "Yo, Moe-B. Make sure them niggas is dead and get the guns."

Moe-B gritted his teeth as he picked up BJ's gun off the ground. The gun felt extra heavy in his hand. He jogged over to where Butta was. He'd been shot, now lying on the ground.

Moe-B didn't see his chest rising and falling, but he shot him in the head anyway. He then ran over to his cousin Lil Tate. He struggled, knowing he really didn't want his cousin's blood on his hands. His hands shook as he stood over him, their eyes making contact. Despite him already being shot, he was alert.

He didn't speak a word as he faced his soon-to-be killer. Moe-B slightly pulled back on the trigger, but only to let up. Tears welled up in his eyes, his top teeth biting down into his bottom lip. Moe-B's hands shook worse than a Parkinson's patient.

"Do it!" Homicide Jack screamed out. Moe-B closed his eyes and squeezed the trigger. Boom!

Honk, honk!

He heard the blaring of the car horn behind his Charger, snapping him back to reality. He took his foot off the break, giving it some gas.

He floated the Charger to the end of the block and parked on the corner to gather his composure. Moe-B wiped the tears he was shedding for his cousin. He knew Lil Tate's actions were nothing but betrayal. But to him, it shouldn't have been penalized by a death sentence even though he tried to help Toflon rob their trap house.

Moe-B and Lil Tate grew up together, their mothers being sisters. He and Tate sometimes shared the same pussy, slept in the same, and broke hard corn bread down the middle when there wasn't enough money between the both of their moms to feed them.

Moe-B wiped his tears as his thoughts went back in time when they were two snotty nose youngins. He remembered how they worked as a team when they were kids stealing out of the neighborhood's grocery store. Wearing oversized Tshirts, they would load their pants with sliced ham and cheese and a loaf of white bread. Moe-B would grab the chips, red juice, and a family size pack of fudge stripe cookies.

Moe-B would then hit the nearest fire alarm and when the store security and store occupants went into a frenzy, they would quickly throw their stolen goods into a used grocery bag and walk right out the store with the rest of the crowd. This was the type of stunts they pulled together to survive in the streets of Bad News, Virginia.

Then out of nowhere, Homicide Jack came on the scene and everything changed for them and their mothers, Rose and Trudie. Homicide Jack became their hero. He made sure their mothers had nice clothes for them and that food stayed on their table. This was how it was when Homicide Jack was in the picture.

One day Rose, Tate's mom, met a young hustler name Trey. Soon, she had fallen deeply in love with. Trey showered Rose with more gifts and money than Homicide Jack had ever done. He promised to take care of Rose and Tate. With her being a helpless romantic, she told her brother she didn't want to be involved in his plots and schemes anymore.

Three months later, Rose and Trey was found dead in his Benz. Both were shot in the head two times each. Shortly after that, Homicide Jack went to jail for a robbery. Tate and Trudie took the death of Rose the hardest. Moe-B didn't know why, but all of sudden the death of Rose put a strain on Homicide Jack and Trudie's relationship. Moe-B and Lil Tate took it as Trudie knowing he had pulled a caper with him in the streets that lead to Rose being killed.

The vibrating phone brought him out of his trance. Wiping more tears from his eyes with the back of his hand, he stared at the caller ID. He saw it was his uncle.

"Hello!"

"Nephew," Homicide Jack's voice came through the phone in a whisper.

"What's good, Doc?"

"I need you to help me get out of this fucking hospital. I'm on papers and if the police find out who I really am, they'll have me violated and I'll be sent back to jail."

"I'm on my way, Unc. Just hold tight."

"Look, when you get here, dial 7-5-7-3-9-9-1-6-1-6. That's my woman, Channtel. She's in the hospital parking lot waiting on you. She'll assist you getting me out of here."

"A'ight, Unc. I'm on it," he said, hitting the end button and disconnecting the call.

Fifteen minutes later, Moe-Be entered the parking lot of Riverside Hospital. He grabbed his phone off his lap and dialed Channtel's number.

"Hello," He heard a sweet voice say, answering the phone.

"Yeah, Channtel? This is Moe-B, Homicide Jack's nephew. I'm in the parking lot. Where are you?"

"I'm on the north side of the parking lot. I'm parked between a red Ford F150 and a navy-blue BMW," she replied.

"Okay, I see you," he stated before getting into her car from the passenger's side. He was impressed by how cute she was, scanning her thighs that threatened to bust out of the seam of her yoga pants. "How are you?"

"I'm good. Just trying to get your uncle out of here."

"A'ight, let's do it then," he told her, watching the parking lot as she exited the car as she made her way towards the hospital. He followed suit, watching her ass bounce the whole time.

Damn, old head kinda fat back there. I see why Unc haven't brought her around to meet the team, he thought to himself. Entering the hospital, they found the waiting area packed with nurses zig-zagging through a sea of sick people as if it was second nature. The chemical smell most hospitals smelled like turned his stomach a little. He followed Channtel who walked through the hospital towards the elevator like she had done this before.

She pressed the call button, opening the elevator doors. The freight was empty. Moe-B stared at her out of the corner of his eye, mesmerized by her. It was nothing special about in particular. Channtel was well proportioned, her B-cups complementing her hips and her hips complementing her thighs and ass. She was tall and shapely, but what made her so beautiful were her gray eyes. She could easily go for Angela Basset but with a set of exotic eyes.

Channtel felt Moe-Be checking her out. "You do know this is a time to be focused and alert, not eyeballing me," she said, breaking the silence and embarrassing the hell out of him. He diverted his eyes and stared straight ahead.

"My bad, Channtel. I'm focused though," he replied. The elevator door opened and the both exited.

"Look for your uncle in room five twenty-two around the corner. Go and get him ready and I'll be there in five minutes," she advised before disappearing down the hall.

Moe-Be made his way towards the room, walking past the nursing station. The nurse was busy talking on the phone and from the sound of it, she was arguing with her lover. Moe-B waked in his hero's room. Homicide Jack sat up in the bed looking more worried than a motherfucking crack head that got caught stealing a hustler's stash.

"What's good, Unc?"

"I'll let you know once I get the fuck out of here. Where the fuck Channtel at?"

"She's coming, Unc. She dipped off somewhere down the opposite end of the hallway.

"Man, them fucking pigs are on their way to see me. The nurse just came in here and told me,' he said with fear in his voice.

"Good afternoon, gentlemen," Channtel said, smiling as she entered the room pushing a wheelchair. She was wearing a powdered blue nursing scrub uniform. She pushed the wheelchair next to the bed, locking the brakes on the wheelchair. This would have been impossible for Channtel to do without Moe-B's assistance. "Go get the elevator, Moe-B. We are right behind you," she instructed him.

When Moe-B left, Channtel leaned over and passionately kissed Homicide Jack. "We almost there, baby," she said, giving him a Colgate smile.

She got behind the wheelchair and pushed her man into the hallway. Her heart was racing harder than a Nascar motor. The nurse that was at the nursing station was nowhere in sight. Channtel felt a little better then. Turning the corner, Moe-B had the elevator door open and ready for them.

Channtel's hands shook as she pushed the button on the elevator that would take them down to the lobby. It seemed like the ride down took forever. Moe-B stared at the numbers above the door that signaled the elevator was descending. Channtel did the same thing as she tapped her foot impatiently.

The freight finally made its destination. Once it did, the doors opened and two detectives entered. The trio froze for a brief second. Channtel then showed her pearly whites and greeted the detectives, batting her gray eyes.

"Hello, Newport News' finest, and when I say that, I do men fine!" she said. The white and black detectives both blushed like two high school kids.

"Good afternoon, ma'am," the black detective spoke, stepping to the side and allowing her to push her pretend patient off of the elevator. "I'm headed to room five twenty-two on the fifth floor. If you get a chance, stop by there and come see me. If not, here's my card." He extended his hand out with a waiting card in it.

Channtel smiled, accepting the detective's card. She walked away, pushing the wheelchair with a little extra in her walk. She knew he was watching. Once the detective had his eyes full of her backside, he let the elevator door close. Channtel peeked over her shoulder to see if the coast was clear, then kindly dropped his card in the nearest trashcan on her way out the door with her man and nephew.

Chapter 4

Moocha had been working at the Riverside Hospital for the last three years. She loved her job, but it was hard work. She had to put in many hours to live a half as decent life. She promised herself she would do whatever it took not to go back to that life she used to live even though her past life had her living life to its fullest. The money and material things weren't worth the loss.

Moocha was a New York, Harlem native. Five years ago, she was the most sought out stripper that left every strip club that she performed in a memorable event and its occupants broke. Standing at a perfect 5'7" with a dark brown complexion, Moocha was of Dominican descendant with full lips and a silky black and curly mane that flowed down her back. She had them mad crazy curves too. Her round bottom was an even forty inches with baby making thighs that only a true Dominican could process. Her plump double C's sat high, begging for attention anytime she step in a room. This beautiful Latin beau favored Jennifer Lopez but was two shades darker and was a thicker version of the singer/actress.

Moocha learned in the strip club how to become cold and turn her emotions off. This was a trait she learned to master over the years. But for some reason, she thought of the woman that was laying in I.C.U. She couldn't get her out of her mind. She gave Vanessa Jones her undivided attention since the first day she laid eyes on her. She didn't know what it was, but when Moocha was around her, she had a feeling they were brought together for a reason. She even felt it without them even communicating as she lied there heavily medicated and in pain.

Vanessa's family hadn't shown up, causing Moocha to wonder why. Moocha desperately wanted to do something for her, so she took it upon herself to go through her belongings and retrieve her phone. She went through her contacts and found a number that had "brother" saved to it. She hit the number that was on speed dial, taking a deep breath. She nervously tapped her foot on the tiled floor as the phone began to ring.

"Vanessa! Where you been? I have been trying to get in touch with you," a voice said coming through the phone. Moocha paused for a few seconds. She was unsure of what to say.

"Ummm, is this Vanessa Jones's brother?" Moocha asked.

"Yeah, who the fuck is this?"

"Please, sir. I could lose my job for doing this, so you can't let my supervisors find out. But I'm a nurse at Riverside Hospital. A few days ago, your sister came in here all shot up."

"What!" BJ shouted through the phone.

"Yeah, she was shot. She's in the I.C.U. unit as we speak. We believe she's going to live but we're not too sure about the baby," Moocha said, running her fingers through her long, silky mane. There was another long pause in the phone. "Hello," Moocha said, thinking that Vanessa's brother hung up.

"I'm here. You said that she's at Riverside Hospital, right?" BJ asked.

"Yeah," she replied.

"A'ight, I'm on my way."

Moocha placed Vanessa's phone back in her belongings and wiped her sweaty palms on her nurse's scrubs. She prayed she had done the right thing by calling her brother. She would find out eventually when he got there.

***

BJ and Tashia fought through the rush hour traffic trying get to Riverside Hospital on the other side of town. A million thoughts ran through BJ's mind. *How the fuck did Vanessa get shot*, he thought to himself. His mind went to Toflon who had recently killed his mother a few months ago. It was in retaliation of BJ killing Toflon's girlfriend, Trici. He wondered was this another move brought on by Toflon.

"Fuck!" he blurred out, breathing hard as he banged his fist against the passenger's side door of Tashia's Benz truck. The outburst startled her, making her jump in her seat as he swerved in and out of lanes.

"Calm down, baby. It's going to be alright. She's going to be okay." Tashia hoped every word she'd just uttered to comfort her man was true. He wasn't trying to hear shit right now. All that was on his mind was Vanessa. He couldn't lose her like he lost his mother. Vanessa was the last sibling he had left.

Pregnant, BJ thought to himself. *My sister is pregnant.* BJ just shook his head and laid it back on the headrest. Two tears drifted down his face. "I'm on my way, sis," he mumbled to himself.

Tashia whipped her Benz truck in the parking lot of Riverside Hospital. She jumped out the truck and rushed around to the passenger's side to help him out the truck. BJ balled his face up in pain as he inched himself out. His ribs were on fire, but nothing in this world could have kept him away from his sister.

Making their way to the entry of the hospital, the double glass doors automatically opened as they approached them. BJ rushed to the nurses' station with Tashia following closely behind.

"Umm, excuse me," he said, interrupting the elderly nurse that occupied the nurse's station as she went over some paper work.

"Yes. How may I help you, young man?"

"Yeah, I just found out that my sister was shot and she's here." His voice cracked as he spoke.

"What's her name, sir?"

"Vanessa Jones."

The nurse started typing on the keyboard of the computer. A few second later, the elderly nurse's facial expression changed. "Sir, Ms. Jones is being treated on the second floor in our Intensive Care Unit. You can go and wait in the waiting room. I'll page the doctor and have him meet you there."

"Is she alright?" he asked with concern in his voice.

"Sir, you will have to speak to the doctor."

"Bitch, I asked you a fucking question. Is my fucking sister okay?" His voice boomed through the lobby waiting area. The hustle and bustle of the hospital seemed to come to a standstill from his sudden outburst. The elderly nurse let out a deep breath and answered him with a shaky voice.

"Sir, please speak with the doctor." Their eyes firmly locked on to one another. Tashia could feel the tension rising as the hospital security made their way to the nurse's station. She didn't want any confrontation, so she intervened.

"Come on, BJ. Let's go and wait for the doctor," she suggested, entwining her arm into his and leading him towards the elevator. She gave the elderly nurse a look of sympathy, mouthing the word "sorry" to her.

Despite the pain he was experiencing, he couldn't sit still. He slowly paced the waiting area floor. Tashia nervously and intensely watched him as she rung her hands together. She was grateful that the Intensive Care Unit's waiting room was empty. She didn't know how he would react once he spoke with the doctor.

She could tell by the elderly nurse's body language and how persistent she was, that he spoke with the doctor about Vanessa.

It had been twenty-five minutes and they were still waiting to see the doctor. Tashia could tell BJ was getting agitated.

"Come over here, baby. Have a seat next to me," Tashia said, trying to get him off his feet. She wanted him to relax, hoping to bring him some type of comfort but he wasn't having it.

He ignored her and kept pacing the floor. A pretty nurse with long, silky hair peeked her head out into the waiting room for the third time in the last fifteen minutes. BJ began to wonder if she was the one that informed him about Vanessa being in the hospital.

"Are you the Jones family?" A lanky, Caucasian man wearing a white lab coat asked us as he walked in the waiting room.

"Yeah, that's us," BJ said, turning around in mid-stride to face the doctor. Tashia got out of her chair, taking his hands into hers as they waited for the doctor to reveal Vanessa's condition.

"I'm Dr. Edelman. What's your relation to Ms. Jones?" he asked, sticking his hand out to greet BJ.

"She's my sister," he replied, taking Dr. Edelman's hand into his.

The doctor removed his Armani glasses and then exhaled. This part of his job he hated the most. Still, it was part of his responsibility, so he had to do it. He looked into BJ's eyes as Tashia gripped his hand tightly. She was bracing herself for the bad news.

"Miss Jones was shot twice. She was struck in the chest, but the bullet was removed. Miraculously, it didn't penetrate deeply into her chest nor did it create any damage to her lungs. It somehow clipped a chain she was wearing during the time of the incident. She also took a shot to the left side of her neck. That bullet was removed, as well." BJ hung on to every word that he said. "She lost a considerable amount of blood."

"Will she be alright?" Tashia asked, interrupting the doctor.

"Well, right now she is stable but she is not out of the woods just yet. We have to make sure no infection sets in her chest where she was shot. We have a draining tube in her chest. We're really concerned about the baby she's carrying through this ordeal."

"Baby?" Tashia blurted out, bringing her hand to her mouth in astonishment.

"What's the situation with the baby?" BJ asked with tears in his eyes. Dr. Edelman briefly broke eye contact with him for a second before responding.

"Well, at this time, we don't know if the baby will make it. Miss Jones was just out of her first trimester."

"Can I see her?" he asked, his voice cracking.

"I'm afraid not, sir. There are no visitors allowed in the I.C.U. wing."

"I want to see my fucking sister!" BJ yelled, snatching his hand away from Tashia.

"It's against our hospital policy. You will only put your sister at risk of getting an infection. A chest infection in her condition will surely kill her," he advised with firmness. BJ began to breathe heavily through his nose.

"Mr. Jones, if your sister is doing well in two days, we'll be moving her to a private room and you can see her there. Until that happens, all you can do is pray and wait." With that, the doctor turned on his heels and exited the waiting room.

BJ took a seat in one of the hospital's light brown chairs that were lined against the wall. He buried his face into the palm of his hands and did something he had never done before. He prayed.

Chapter 5

Three days later, Homicide Jack stretched his 5'8", lanky frame across his black leather sofa. He was relieved to be away from the hospital and in the comfort of his own home. He was deeply in need of a shave. The stubs of hair that sprouted out his baldhead and around his face gave him a five o'clock shadow that made him appear to be older than what he truly was.

Homicide Jack was a motor oil complexion. Lying against the black leather made him and the sofa blend in somewhat perfectly. Channtel had been taking care of him like she was a licensed nurse. She changed his bandages, gave him sponge baths, made sure he took his pain meds and she even sucked his dick to take the edge off him. Channtel did everything possible to help him cope and recover from his gunshot wounds. The one he received in the shoulder didn't bother him as much, but the surgery he had to remove the bullet from his hip was a muthafucka. It bothered him nonstop. He decided once he healed and could move around, he was going to locate Toflon and kill him with his bare hands for all the fucking pain he caused him.

He rubbed his hand over the shoulder where he was shot. He felt the area around the wound. It was somewhat tender and stiff. He let out a deep sigh. Then he grabbed the remote that rested on his stomach and started flicking channels on the Sony T.V. He stopped on the Jerry Springer show.

He remembered many days in prison watching ole Jerry Springer exploit the lives of his guests by providing a platform right on national television where they aired out their bizarre and mischievous dealings and dirty laundry. Homicide Jack chuckled at the two, white oversized truck drivers that looked at bitches going at it in a twerk contest.

Knock, knock, knock!

The knocks on the door diverted his attention from his show. He turned the volume down and forced himself to sit up on the sofa. The leather stuck to his back from him lying down on it the majority of the day. He pulled a white V-Neck T-shirt over his head, placing his 45 on a nearby coffee table under his right leg.

"Channtel, get the door for me!" he yelled out to her. She was in the other room of her one-bedroom apartment doing her wifey duties, ironing and folding clothes. Channtel strutted out the room barefoot, wearing a wife beater that was slightly transparent. It showed a glimpse of her Hershey Kisses shaped nipples that were pressed against it fabric. He grabbed a handful of his manhood through his jeans, watching her with a sexual hunger in his eyes.

Since he escaped from the hospital, his hip was too sore for them to be intimate but Channtel had been blessing him with some superb head every night before bed. He made a mental note in the back of his mind to get into her guts later on that night.

"Who is it?" she asked, peeping out through the peephole of the door.

"LJ!" he said.

Homicide Jack was expecting his old crime buddy. LJ had called an hour earlier letting him know that he was stopping by. Homicide Jack was angry with LJ. He gave him a job to do about a month ago and LJ had failed to complete the job. He started to avoid his calls. Channtel opened the door and let him in, closing the door behind him. She made her exit, leaving Homicide Jack and LJ alone to talk in private.

"Homicide, what's good, my nigga?" LJ said, greeting him.

"You tell me. You've been avoiding my calls after I gave you my fucking money," Homicide Jack barked sternly.

LJ stood at even 6'0", weighing in at 165 pounds. He had an athletic physique. He could pass as a Samuel L. Jackson but with a set of light green eyes. He also possessed some oversized hands, the kind often seen on dope fiends.

"Yo, Homicide. You have to forgive me for that. I had to block everything out and get focused. You were blowing a nigga phone up, making them weak ass indirect threats. I had to tune everything out and get the job done," LJ stated, looking firmly at him.

"Nigga, what indirect threats? There ain't nothing indirect about nothing I say!" he yelled, causing him to feel some pain in his hip. "I paid you my fucking money for a job. When I call your ass, you need to answer the fucking phone. And you still haven't handled your business."

He looked at Homicide like he was a two-headed snake. He was fucked up at how he was talking to him like he was some chump and not a man.

"Yo, Homicide. Watch your tone, homeboy. Just know the job has been taken cared of. That shit was done five days ago," he told him with a smirk on his face.

"I'm in my fucking house and I speak the way I please up in this bitch. Don't ever get that twisted. And you haven't took care of shit because I haven't heard shit about 40 being dead," he said a little loud, causing Channtel to peek her head out of the bedroom, gripping a chrome .38.

LJ caught her appearance, while Homicide Jack's head gesture denied her assistance.

"My nigga, I took care of that shit five days ago," he said, removing a Black and Mild from his front pocket. He took a seat in the matching leather recliner that sat on the left side of the sofa.

Homicide Jack studied his friend's face and saw the truth in his eyes. He thought about what LJ had said. He took care of that about five days ago. He realized he might have not heard about it because he was laid up in the hospital and now home recuperating. "Damn, LJ. My bad. I've been under so much stress lately. A nigga tried to take me off the earth a few days ago," he said, revealing his shoulder to him that was covered with a bandage from the gunshot would.

"Man, what the fuck!" he said, lighting his Black and Mild.

"Yeah, we had a crazy ass gun battle over there on twenty-fourth street. I got hit twice, so I've been out of commission for the last couple of days. That's probably why I haven't heard about the hit, but are you sure you killed him?" he asked.

LJ chuckled. "Does a stripper love a pole? I put one in his face and dropped the bitch he was with on GP," he boasted.

"Bitch? What bitch you talking about?" he inquired.

"Man, he had some fine ass brown-skinned bitch with him. I hated to do it to her, but you know I can't leave any witnesses behind. I wish I could have fucked her. Geesh! That bitch was fine,' he said, laughing.

Homicide Jack sat back and thought about the situation. He was hoping he didn't kill the broad who was with 40. That would be something that could cause additional problems for him and BJ.

"Yo, Homicide. Are you going to need some help with your situation?" he asked, pointing to his injured shoulder. "Because you know a nigga could use some more scrilla."

"Naw, I'm coolin' on that. The young nigga that did this is a dead man walking," he replied with fire in his yes.

"Well, a'ight then. Let me get the other half of my money for the business you owe me. I got shit I need to handle in a major way."

"Yeah, hold up a minute. Hey, Channtel. Look in the closet on the top shelf and bring me that brown bag," he yelled. She came out of the room wearing the same attire from earlier. LJ watched closely at her body, especially her thighs.

Damn this broad is fly as hell, he thought to himself. He smirked and looked away as she gave him a dirty look. She didn't like the fact that he had upset her man. She handed him the money and quickly made her exit.

"It's fifteen thousand in here," he told him, handing him the bag. "The ten is what's owed to you. The other five is just for good measure for dropping the broad. But next time I put you on a move and you duck out on me and not check in, then consider that your last move," he stated firmly, making eye contact with LJ.

"Yeah, Homicide Jack. I gotcha. But when am I going to meet the boss? I'm ready to eat!"

"As soon as I'm able to get up and move around," he replied.

"Okay, that sounds like a plan," he said, standing up and giving Homicide Jack some dap. "Hit me on the phone if you need me. I'm going to lay low and get me a place and some wheels. But I'll be waiting on you to hit me on when it's a good time to meet up with BJ," he told him, making his way to the door.

Homicide Jack felt a little relieved knowing that 40 was somewhere taking a dirt nap and out of the hair of BJ. He reached for his phone lying next to him and dialed his number. The phone rang three times before he answered it.

"Hello."

"What's up, young buck?" Homicide Jack said. BJ instantly noticed his voice.

"Ain't too much. I'm just headed to the hospital to see my sister."

"Is Vanessa okay?" he asked with concern in his voice.

"Right now, I really don't know. This is my first time seeing her since she's been out of the I.C.U. unit."

"What the fuck happened to her?"

"Homicide Jack, some sucka ass nigga shot her," he told him, choking up.

"Damn!' he replied, grabbing a Newport 1000 out of its pack and putting some heat to the cigarette.

"Do you think it was Toflon?" Homicide Jack asked.

"Man, I don't know. Most likely since he was the one that killed my mother." Homicide Jack paused and thought on that for a minute.

"Listen, I got some news for you," he told him.

"Okay, spill it."

"Remember ole boy, 40?"

"Yeah, I remember." BJ perked up hearing 40's name.

"Well, that little lotto ticket has been cashed in on him," he said with a smirk on his face.

"Oh yeah?" BJ said, smiling. "Yo, Homicide Jack. I'm just now pulling up at the hospital. Let me get back at you later. We can talk about this later but good looking out. Toflon is next, you hear me."

"I hear ya, young blood. Be safe," he said to him, disconnecting the call. He laid his back on the cushion of the sofa and took a deep breath. He took a pull of his nicotine stick as he thought about how shit would play out. He knew he was going to have to make his exit out of the game sooner than later. His mind jumped to Channtel in them sweatpants and immediately, his dick got hard. It was time to test his him out. "Chann, come here and let me see you for a minute," he said with a smile.

Chapter 6

BJ stepped through the glass sliding doors of the Riverside Hospital. His stomach had the butterflies. He tried to compose himself but he was way too nervous. The hospital staff called him this morning. They informed him that earlier that morning, Vanessa had been placed in a private room on the fifth floor in room 524.

He made his way to the gift shop, purchasing two dozen of red and blue balloons with the words "Get Well" and a smiley face logo stamped on them. He also purchased a cream-colored teddy bear that held a heart in its arm that had the words "I Love You".

BJ paid the cashier for his purchase and paid the young, barely legal gift shop worker an extra ten dollars to bring the balloons up to her in an hour. He took the bear under his arm, slowly making his way to the elevator. He still experienced some pain in his ribs, but the pain in his heart couldn't be compared.

He made Tashia stay at home while he went to see Vanessa. She protested and pouted as he left her behind. He honestly didn't know what to expect when he saw Vanessa, so he thought it was best to see her alone. Then he would call Tashia to come join him later.

Getting on the elevator, BJ hit the call button that sent the elevator up to the fifth floor. He leaned his back against the freight wall and sighed at the ceiling, wondering and contemplating on the words of the infamous Notorious B.I.G, "More Money, More Problems."

All of this was taking place in his life because he was getting money and another nigga wanted to take it. *I guess this is the type of shit that happens when the streets clapped back,* BJ thought to himself. He didn't even have these types of problems when he was broke. He shook his head at the thought.

The elevator stopped on the fifth floor, letting BJ out. He made his way to the nurse's station. "Umm, excuse me. Could you point me in the right direction to room five twenty-four?" BJ asked a young blond man that was manning the desk dressed in some crisp pink nursing scrubs.

"Who are you here to see, sir?" he asked with a smile.

"My sister, Vanessa Jones," BJ replied.

"Okay, her room is located down this hall. It's the second door on the right at the end of the hall."

"Thanks," BJ replied, giving the nurse a weak smile.

BJ took the bear from under his arm and smoothed its fur out as he made his way down the corridor. He had no problem locating Vanessa's room. He walked in, stumbling on weak knees after seeing his big sister hooked up to so many machines. Every wire and tube known to man was running from her body.

The thumping in his chest felt like a horse had double kicked him in his chest. BJ eased towards her with tears welling up in his eyes, causing a river of salty tears to run down his face. He felt like he could barely breath.

"Sis." BJ's voice got caught in his throat, his tongue becoming dry as number five sand paper. He placed the teddy bear under her arm and held her hand. She looked small and frail, making him want to wrap her in his arms, shielding her from the world. Brushing a few strains of loose hair from her face, BJ leaned over and kissed his sister's forehead, leaving traces of his tears behind.

"I'm here, sis," BJ managed to say in the form of a whisper. "I'm here, big sis." He stroked her face with the back of his hand. "A nigga is going to pay with his life for this." He already had made up his mind that he was going to kill everybody that was associated with Toflon. BJ gritted his teeth in frustration. "Grrrrr!"

His eyes drifted down to Vanessa's belly, placing a trembling hand on her stomach. BJ fell to his knees and started to weep. It broke his heart to see his pregnant sister in this state. He had just lost his mother and now Vanessa was laying on her deathbed.

"Oops, excuse me. I'll come back later," a beautiful nurse said from the doorway, turning on her heels to leave.

BJ immediately recognized her as the nurse that kept peeping her head in and out the I.C.U.'s waiting room the other day.

"Hold up! Wait!" he yelled out her, struggling to get to his feet. The nurse saw him grappling in pain to get up. She rushed over to him to help him to his feet.

"Are you alright, sir?

"Yeah, I'm cool," BJ said, straightening out his Versace shirt. He stepped back from the nurse and read the nametag that said, "Nurse Gomez".

"Go ahead and handle your business," he told her.

"Are you sure? I could come back later," she insisted.

"Naw, it's cool."

"Okay," she replied. She started checking the machines, making sure they were working properly. She also changed the drainage bag that was received liquids from her chest. She replaced it with a fresh bag, then changed the bandages on Vanessa's chest. BJ stood there, watching Nurse Gomez's every move.

"Thanks for calling me. If you hadn't, I would have even known she was here," he said, sticking his cold hands inside of his jeans pockets. Nurse Gomez froze.

"Please, not here. I go on break in ten minutes. Let's talk in the cafeteria," she insisted.

BJ nodded his head up and down in agreement. He continued to watch Nurse Gomez attending to his sister with tender loving care. He could tell she was good at what she did. She threw the soiled bandage away and latex gloves in the red hazardous container under the sink. Once done, she properly washed her hands and led him to the cafeteria.

***

40 passed Nurse Gibblings the folded paper that he scribbled a few words on. She studied the note with apprehension. She

knew it was against the hospital's policy for patients to make patient-to-patient visits. If caught by the right shift supervisor, she could be suspended or even fired.

***

"Mr. Pulley, I cannot act on this request," she said, shaking her head side to side.

"Pleassse!" 40 begged through wired shut jaws."

Nurse Gibblings looked into his pleading eyes. It was breaking her heart. All she could see was a man desperately wanting to see about the well-being of his woman and unborn child. She believed everything happened for a reason. And the reason they were both placed on the same floor was a true testament to her belief in God. To her, he wanted them both there.

***

Nurse Gomez and BJ sat in the corner of the small cafeteria. She had a turkey and cheese sub with a bottled water. BJ had an apple juice.

"So, Ms. Gomez. Why did you call me for my sister?" he asked.

"Please call me, Moocha," she said, correcting him.

"Moocha? What type of mane is that? That sounds like a striper name or something?" BJ said, smiling.

"I'll tell you about it at a later date and a different place because this is not the place," she replied.

"Okay, then. I can respect that, but call me BJ."

Moocha stared at him for a second, taking in his features. He was a little cutie, a little young but definitely a cutie. She had observed his attire and the diamond Cartier watch he sported on his arm. She knew then he was in contact with some money. Her background had taught her how to pinpoint things like that. She didn't want this stranger to think she was out to get a come up on him, so in this situation, she chose to just tell the truth.

"Well, I have seen her lying in that I.C.U. unit for two whole days. Not a soul called or came to check up on that beautiful girl. I just knew she had to have someone out there that cared about her. I felt like she needed the support of her family and loved ones. So, I went through her belongings and found her phone, went through her contacts and came across your number. The rest is history," she said, swiping a few loose strands of hair out of her face as she took a drink out of her water bottle.

BJ nodded his head up and down as a sign of respect. "You got an accent, Moocha. Where are you from?"

"From the Dominican Republic, but I represent Harlem, papi," she said with a little hood flavor, letting him know she could be hood if she needed to be.

"Okay, that explains it,' he said with a smile.

"Explains what?" Moocha inquired.

"Your wittiness," he replied, finishing off his can of apple juice. "Listen, Moocha. I like your vibes and I appreciate you calling me." BJ dug in his pocket of his Versace jeans and removed a jumbled-sized knot, peeling off 20 one hundred-dollar bills. Here's two Gs."

"Oh no! I can't accept that," she said, sitting straight up, looking around the cafeteria to see if anyone was watching.

"Naw, ma. You got to take it. I'm a man that don't take too kindly to people telling me no." Moocha knew she could use the money, but she protested against it anyway.

"I'm sorry, but I can't." BJ discreetly pushed the money across the table to her. Moocha hesitated before he placed his hand over her small hand, leaving the stack of money in it. She slowly closed it before placing her it in her pocket.

"So, tell me my sister going to be okay? Keep it real with me," he asked. Moocha heard the concern of a true brother in his voice.

"With time and some loving care, she's going to be fine. I got her. She's in good hands. Trust me, I have seen a lot of others worse off that bounce back from it."

"I hope so because I'm leaving you responsible for my sister," BJ said sternly.

"How you just gone put that big responsibility on my plate like it's nothing?" she stated seriously.

BJ put his head down. "I'm sorry, Moocha. I just want my sister to be alright."

"And I can understand that. I promise I will do whatever I can for your sister. But you need to stay off your ribs for a while, the ones you're over there nursing," she said, pointing to BJ's right hand he had placed over his left rib.

"I will once I know that sister is going to be alright," he replied.

"Well, my break is over. I have to get back to my floor. Come on, let me get you back to your sister," she said with a smile. Moocha stood and cleared off the table they shared as they made their way out of the cafeteria. BJ followed behind her, admiring the way her panties were biting into her round backside.

***

Nurse Gibblings eased 40 into the corridor in a wheelchair. She let him convince her to wheel him down the hall to see Vanessa. She was so nervous, but knowing she was at least twenty-five feet away from her room brought her some comfort. She knew that taking him to go see her was doable without being caught.

40's hands broke out in a sweat. He became slightly dizzy. The anticipation of seeing her was unbearable, the closer he was wheeled to her room. His heart started thumping hard in his chest like a bass drum. Nurse Gibblings made a quick left, turning into her room. She rolled him next to her bed and locked the wheelchair brakes.

"Mr. Pulley, you have exactly five minutes and not an extra minute longer. I'll be right back," she said sternly like a mother would tell her small child. With that, she turned on her heels and disappeared out the door.

He couldn't believe his eyes. The scene that was before him was horrifying. He could never imagine Vanessa looking so frail and helpless. He didn't fight his tears, letting them easily flow as rage boiled inside his inner core. He leaned up and softly touched her arm. He wanted to give her some type of comfort. He wanted to let her know that he was there for her.

Her arm felt cold and damp under his touch. He wished he could talk to her, but that was impossible to do with a wired shut jaw. He placed his hand on Vanessa's baby bump. The thought of her losing the baby was frightening to him. Tears continued to flow from his eyes.

He felt her stir in bed. He looked up and saw her eyes open. He gave her the best smile he could manage despite the pain it caused him in his face.

The monitor started beeping and going haywire. Moments later, nurses and doctors rushed the room. "Excuse me, sir. You don't belong in here. You have to go back to your room," said a nurse, rushing over to Vanessa's bedside.

"I got him," Nurse Gibblings said, grabbing hold of the handles to 40's wheelchair and push him out the room. He tried to protest, but it fell on deaf ears. He was protesting so much that he didn't see BJ step in front of his wheelchair. Both of their eyes met which held nothing but pure hatred.

Seeing all the commotion going on behind 40 drove BJ insane. "Bitch ass nigga, it was you! You did this!" BJ yelled, catching 40 with a Mike Tyson right hook. He knocked him out the wheelchair, reawakening the fresh raw pain in 40's jaw. The nurse and doctors had to restrain him from causing any more damage. They helped 40 back into his wheelchair. Nurse Gibblings continued to escort 40 back to his room. He needed to be prepped for the doctor to examine his jaw for further injuries. BJ continued to fight to get at 40.

"Listen, young man. If you continue to conduct yourself in that manner, the hospital will have to arrest you," one of the doctors warned him. BJ couldn't afford to go to jail right now. He needed to know what was going on with Vanessa. Then he would inform Homicide Jack that 40 was still existing among the living.

Chapter 7

The bittersweet purp Fever inhaled in his lungs helped to dull some of the pain and stress from losing his brother, Butta. However, the drug only helped to a small degree. He let the smoke out his lungs along with a deep sigh. He shook his head at the thought of seeing his brother in a casket the day before. He knew Butta was in the streets living by the gun. He also knew that if anyone lived their life in that manner, surely, they would die by it.

Fever being a certified street nigga himself, respected the code of the streets, but Butta was his brother. He couldn't allow that situation to go unchecked. There were too many eyes on him. There wasn't a nigga in the city of Newport News big enough to drop his brother and not go untouched.

Avenging his brother's death was a must. He secretly blamed Toflon. He wasn't ready to expose his hand until he could find out who the nigga BJ was. Then and only then would he kill Toflon for having his brother out there on some bullshit.

Fever had that pustule type of acne. He resembled the rapper Craig Mack, but just a chubbier version. He even had the big lips to match. Standing at 5'8", Fever wore his 258-pound frame well. He had hazel green eyes that changed colors when he became angry. He rocked a low Caesar cut. He was a straight hot head, too. He loved to fight and bang his gun on anyone that wronged him.

Fever's temper always ran hot, so that's how he got his name. However, more than violence, Fever loved money. He and his crew controlled a nice portion of the purp that came into Newport News. He wanted Butta to join him in his small empire, but he wasn't with the hustling. His motto was "why hustle all day when you could take the money off the niggas that hustle all day".

Fever hit the purp stuffed in a Black and Mild again and passed it to Toflon. "So, what's up with the nigga that killed my brother?" he asked him.

"I'm trying to get a line on the nigga, fam. The nigga is laying low. I know I put two in him, so the nigga must have been wearing vest or some shit. I really can't get out there and smoke the nigga out because shit's way too hot out there right," Toflon replied, accepting the Black and Mild from Fever, pulling from it.

"Yeah, I'm on it though. Just give me a minute. I'm going to drop a hundred rounds the next time I get a chance to get the drop on BJ," Toflon boasted, letting smoke seep out his nose.

Fever rolled his eyes in irritation. He was fighting hard not to draw the Glock from his hip and push Toflon's shit all over the wall behind him. Toflon could feel the ill vibes that he was giving off. He knew hands to hands he couldn't fuck with Fever, but when it came to that gunplay, Toflon felt he had a chance.

Toflon deeply despised Fever because he thought a nigga couldn't lay his ass down in the streets. He felt no one had the nuts to try him and take what he had, but Toflon knew *anyone* could get it. But what made Toflon really hate him was Fever laughing in their face after him and Butta asked to run security for him. Instead, he wanted to give them a couple of pounds and a block to hustle on for him. They both declined, continuing to get their money the fast way, the ski mask way.

"I got a move for you if you interested," Fever said, wiping the extra spit from his big lips. He was offering him a job to keep him around long enough to rock him to sleep.

"Oh yeah? What that lick read?" Toflon ears perked up hearing the mention of a lick.

"Four hundred pounds of the best weed Cali has to offer."

"Fever, no disrespect but you know I'm not with that hustling shit," Toflon complained.

"Well, you should because the stick-up game hasn't been good to you or my brother," he said with a frown on his face.

"But I tell you what. The caper pays one hundred thousand in cash," he told him reaching for the burning Black and Mild in Toflon's hand.

Toflon's ears started popping after hearing how much his payout would be for the job.

"I'm in nigga. So, where I sign up at?" Toflon asked, smiling.

"I'm going to put you down in a few days," Fever said, hitting the weed.

"Okay, tell me at least who the nigga is," Toflon said. Fever looked at him like he was stupid.

"It's a nigga that's so high in the weed chain that you couldn't even get close enough to buy a pound of weed from. But I'll tell you this," Fever said, licking his big lips. "The nigga cut me out a deal that we were supposed to make together, so it's time for me to get my fair share of the deal," he said with a wicked grin on his face.

"A'ight, I can respect that," Toflon said, giving Fever a pound on the fist. "Well, hit me on the hip and give me the business about the move but know that I'm with it," he told him, standing up to leave.

"Be safe out there in them streets bending them corners." Fever got up and followed Toflon to the door, giving him another pound.

"Make sure you get at me when you hear something about that nigga BJ."

"Most definitely. I'm going to let you know something," Toflon said as Fever closed the door behind him. Fever sat back down in his recliner and thought about the current situation. He had too much going to wait on Toflon's bitch ass to find BJ. He needed results ASAP. Therefore, an idea came to mind. Once he used Toflon to help him grab the four hundred pounds, he would have him drop it. But for now, he needed to place a call to his clean up man. Fever grabbed the phone off the arm of the recliner and punched a few numbers into the phone. The person picked up on the second ring.

"Hello," a raspy voice said.

"Yo, LJ, this is Fever."

"What's the business." LJ replied.

"You know a nigga name BJ?" There was a pause on the phone.

"I've haven't met him but I've heard of him."

"Well, I need to meet with you about him. It's a fifty piece on it if you're interested?" Fever told him, letting him know he had a $50,000 check on BJ's head.

"Ain't no muthafuckin' question if I'm interested," LJ said.

"Well, we'll meet at the IHOP for brunch tomorrow afternoon."

"A'ight, say no more," LJ said, disconnecting the call. Fever sat back in his recliner and sparked another purp stuffed with Black and Mild. He closed his eyes as he thought about his brother Butta. "This one's for you, bruh."

***

Toflon drove his Acura down Madison headed towards Blue Liquid. He was in the mood to see some big titties and ass. He really didn't know what to make of the meeting with Fever. He could sense Fever was mad at him or thought he was the reason Butta got killed.

"Naw, if that was the case, Fever would have tried to kill me right there on the spot." Toflon shook that thought out of his mind, instead thinking about the one hundred thousand dollars at stake for the caper. He'd been waiting for a lick like this to come a long for a minute now.

He just wished Butta were there to go on the mission with him. If Butta were still alive, he would've felt a whole lot better going into the situation. He knew Fever wouldn't try anything if Butta were alive. Something just didn't sit right for him and he knew from the past that Fever couldn't be trusted.

Turning into the parking lot of Blue Liquid, Toflon made up his mind he was going to play Fever close. This way he could see what he could pick up on him. That's all he could do now. He just hoped and prayed he didn't have to kill Fever or worse, let Fever kill him.

Chapter 8

This morning was a real scary one for BJ. He thought for sure that when he saw Vanessa's body shake and jerked the way that it did, he'd lost her. He learned she had a seizure due to the pain medications administrated to her. BJ's mind was in overdrive. He found out through Moocha that Vanessa and 40 came to the hospital together clinging to their lives by a thread. He found out 40 was supposedly the father of her unborn child.

Shit was too close to home. BJ had to make some harsh decisions. There was no way he could let 40 live knowing he had vowed to kill him. BJ shook his head at the thought. He sat in Riverside Hospital's parking lot thinking about his next move. He wondered if Vanessa loved that nigga 40. He remembered the times she mentioned she was in love, but it was with some with named Rob. He found out Rob was Robert A.K.A 40.

"Fuck! Fuck!" he screamed out, banging his hand on the Charger's steering wheel. BJ was so mad that he wanted to hurt someone. Homicide Jack entered his mind. *If this nigga would have handled that hit personally, Vanessa wouldn't be up in the hospital and 40 would be somewhere taking a dirt nap*, BJ thought to himself.

He wasn't thinking clearly, anger clouding his thoughts. BJ took the Glock 40 from underneath the driver's seat and brought the Charger to life.

***

"Damn, nephew. Where you get this shit from? This weed is good than a muthafuka!" Homicide asked in between pulls of the backwoods.

"You like that, Unc? That's that purp them Fever boys be selling on Jefferson Avenue by Magic City," Moe-B told him.

"True bill, nephew. This some good shit. So, what brings you through here?" he asked him, putting the ashes from the backwoods into a nearby ashtray.

"Ain't nothing. I'm just checking up on you, that's all," he said, but really he wanted to talk about Lil Tate. He just hadn't built up enough courage to do it yet

"You know you could have just call, right?" Homicide Jack said, pushing to get his nephew to spill what was on his mind. He wasn't too happy about unexpected visitors just showing up at his house, family or not. "How's business out there since it's you and Bugg is out there holding everything down right now? Homicide Jack inquired, still enjoying the purp.

"Since we lost the trap on twenty-fourth street, shit's been slow. But the other spot is making money, just as much as we used to," Moe-B confessed. Homicide Jack nodded his up and down, confirming he understood the situation.

"That's why you can't do both. It's even money or war. War always fucks up the money," Homicide Jack said, passing the weed back to Moe-B. "I'll be back in no time. Just keep that trap house open twenty-four seven and keep them niggas on point. Don't let up. Work them niggas until they fall flat on their faces."

"I gotcha, Unc," said Moe-B. He knew if he didn't say something about Lil Tate now, he never would never. "Aye, Unc. I want to holla at you about Lil Tate.

Boom, boom, boom!

The knocks coming from the front door sounded like the police knocking. They startled them and even Channtel came running out the room looking confused.

"Who the fuck is that?" Channtel asked through the door, looking out the peephole.

"It's BJ! Open up, Channtel."

BJ's voice could be heard clearly through the door. Channtel looked over her shoulder towards Homicide Jack for guidance. He nodded his head up and down, giving her the okay to open the door. Once she did, BJ stepped in.

"Damn, young blood. You knocking like you the fuck—" Homicide Jack's words froze in his throat when he saw BJ clutching the Glock 40. He gritted his teeth in rage, swiftly cocking the slider back that placed a slug into the chambers with a loud metallic click clack sound.

"Whoa, whoa! What's this all about?" he questioned him slowly, raising his hands in the air.

"This shit is about my sister. It's because of you she's in the hospital holding on to her life by a fucking thread!" BJ yelled in rage. Homicide looked confused.

"BJ, what the fuck you talking about?" he asked with his hands still in the air.

"Whoever you sent to kill 40, shot my sister too. I paid you to handle that shit for me." BJ gripped the Glock tighter. Chantel was frozen in fear while Moe-B eased his hand to his hip where his .357 rested. Shit was starting to make sense for Homicide Jack. He remembered LJ saying he shot a broad that was with 40 when he made the hit.

"BJ, put the gun down and let's figure this shit out like partners are supposed to do," Homicide Jack pleaded.

"Man, fuck that! Who was the shooter? Who you hired to take the hit?" BJ asked.

"Why?" Homicide Jack questioned.

"Because that muthafucka is a dead man. 40 still alive and that bitch ass nigga almost killed my sister."

"Listen to me, BJ. Put the hammer down." Homicide Jack could see his nephew easing towards his gun. "No!" he screamed, instructing Moe-B to stand down. "Young blood, we all on the same team. There has to be some type of mix up. I know you're hurting and have every right to be. I love Vanessa just like you do, but you got to put the gun down and let's talk about this shit," he said in a sincere voice, trying to bring BJ back from off the edge of no return. Everything he said was starting to set in with BJ.

"Everyone, get the fuck out!" BJ yelled with tears in his eyes.

Channtel and Moe-B hesitated. "Now!" he shouted.

Moe-B wasn't going to leave his uncle behind but Homicide nodded his head towards the door, letting him know he wanted him to leave, as well. Moe-B got up and gave BJ a cold stare, making his way to the door with Channtel on his heels.

"Who was the nigga that shot my sister?" BJ asked.

"First, drop the burner and let's talk," he said from the sofa with his hands still in the air. "Is this really about me and you or is this about someone making a mistake? I didn't even know this took place," he told him in a serious tone.

BJ knew Homicide Jack was right. He lowered his weapon, letting it hang loosely in his hand by his right leg. Relief came over Homicide Jack once he saw he didn't have him in the sights of his gun.

"Have a seat, young blood. Let's talk." BJ took a seat in the recliner where Moe-B sat just moments ago. BJ held that predatory animal-like look in his eyes. His face was still full of anger.

"I found out today at the hospital that Vanessa was with 40 the night your man shot him." BJ paused, wiping his left hand, still clutching the Glock in his right one. Homicide Jack broke out in goose bumps after he heard this.

BJ continued. "I went to see my sister today at the hospital and when I came back from the cafeteria, 40 was in Vanessa's room. I thought he was behind my sister being shot, so I attacked him. I learned from the nurse they were brought together and to put stink on shit, Vanessa is pregnant with his child," he said, getting up from the recliner and pacing the floor. "I can't let this nigga live, Homicide," BJ said more to himself as he moved back and forth across the living room floor. He dragged his hand over his face, while swinging the Glock by his side. "40 already told Tashia he was out to kill me for Skalez's murder."

"Tashia? BJ, I know you don't have that woman in your business," Homicide Jack said, relaxing back on the sofa. On the inside, he was livid. He came into his home and upped a strap on him, but he decided to deal with that later.

"Tashia has always been in the mix before we even knew she was in the mix," BJ replied. "She overheard me asking you to kill 40."

"What! BJ, I don't play them type of games," Homicide Jack told him, sitting back up on the edge of the sofa, looking nervous. He pulled a cigarette out the Newport 100 pack that was on the table in front of him, lighting one up.

"Man, don't trip but it goes deeper than that," BJ said as he kept pacing the floor. "Tashia was there that night Skalez, Block, 40 and me pulled the caper on the nigga Lance. Matter of fact, she was the one that set the whole thing up."

"BJ, this shit is like some twisted tale out one of the urban books that's published through Lock Down Publications I read when I was doing time upstate," Homicide Jack said, taking a long pull off his Newport, running his hand over his studded bald head. "So, what we going to do, BJ?"

"I really don't know right now," he replied, stopping in the middle of the floor as he slightly tapped the Glock against his leg. Homicide Jack's phone then rang.

"Hello."

"Unc, everything alight in there?" Moe-B asked him through the phone, standing on the opposite side of the apartment door with a worried Channtel.

"I'm good, Nephew. Take care of Channtel. Go get something to eat and I'll call you in a hour," he instructed him before ending the call. "Yo, BJ. Let me take care of this 40 shit. You just make sure Tashia keep her cool and I'm going to fix it. Just give me a chance, young blood," he asked, taking another pull of his burning cigarette

BJ shook his head in frustration. "Now that I know my sister is pregnant by 40, I don't know if she will understand if he end up dead. After all, that's her child's father." BJ was trying to rationalize within himself, but Homicide Jack wasn't having it.

"Man, fuck that! You think that nigga is going to let up off you once he gains his bearings? He's going to hit back and he's going to hit back hard," he barked, staring at BJ like he was crazy. BJ knew he was right.

"So, you advise we move forward?" BJ asked.

"Without a doubt!"

"A'ight, they moved 40 to the second floor. They wanted to keep us apart. He's in room two eleven. I got a nurse that works there that can keep tabs on him for us. When he's released, we'll be right there," BJ said, plotting and stargazing. "We can follow him to his crib and make a move. That shouldn't be hard too hard to do since he has a bullet in the foot and a broken arm and jaw. He'll be a easy target," he said with a smirk on his face, thinking about 40 finally being out the way.

Homicide Jack moved his head up and down in agreement, stubbing out the cigarette in the ashtray.

"That's it, young blood. Use your head and stop moving with your emotions. They'll cause you to make mistakes like coming into a man's home and pulling a gun on him," he said through clenched teeth.

BJ locked eyes with Homicide Jack and said, "My bad."

"Your bad? Your bad don't erase the transgression that was committed," he replied firmly. "But a pass is warranted in this matter since you looked out for me when you didn't even know me. But there will be no other time because the next time you lift that gun on me, make sure you squeeze that shit until its empty," he told him as they still held eye contact with each other.

BJ clearly heard the warning coming out of his mouth. The glare he saw in Homicide Jack's eyes let him know this act should never happen again. "I understand, Homicide. That shit will never happen again." BJ walked over to him and gave him some dap.

Homicide Jack respected BJ's heart, viewing him like a son, but he knew if he ever pulled another gun on him, he would have no choice but to kill him. Homicide Jack struggled to get to his feet. Still suffering from his gunshot wounds, he embraced BJ with a hug of a father. "Let's get this situation cleared up before it gets further outta control," he said, releasing BJ.

"Yeah, let's do it," BJ replied, feeling a little better about the current situation. He made his way to the door and paused.

"Yo, Homicide. Thanks for the pass."

Homicide Jack smiled lightly. "You're welcome, but know you don't get another one," he stated firmly. BJ hesitated then nodded his head up and down as he made his way out the door.

Chapter 9

A rhythmically pain throbbed throughout Vanessa's body as she sluggishly opened her eyes. Her surroundings were dark.

Beep, beep, beep.

The constant pitch of the machines around her was all she could hear. *Where am I?* she thought to herself. Her lungs felt empty of air as she fought to breathe deeply. Her heart rate elevated dramatically as fear grabbed a hold of her body. Vanessa's throat was so dry that it burned. She wanted so badly to call out for help, but the dryness in her throat wouldn't allow her.

The machines beeping amplified. Soon she heard the sounds of people rushing into the room. A nurse and a doctor wearing a white lab coat came in and immediately went to work checking her vitals.

"Ms. Jones, please try to relax," the beautiful Hispanic nurse said in a caring tone, trying to smooth her out of her panic state.

The doctor checked the reading on the monitor. "Ms. Jones, do you know where you are?" the nurse asked her. Vanessa tried to talk but shook her head to left and right. She stuck her tongue out. The nurse then could see the dry whiteness that burdened her tongue. Instantly, she knew she needed some water.

She grabbed the water pitcher with the crushed ice in it from the stand next to the bed. She poured Vanessa some water in a paper cup, placing it up to parched lips. "There you go," she said, coaching her.

Vanessa tried to drink fast. "Take your time, Ms. Jones. We have plenty of water," she told her, dabbing away the access water that dripped from her mouth. The water seemed to bring life to her tongue. The nurse gave her a few more sips of water.

"Hello, Ms. Jones. I'm Dr. Edelman. You are at Riverside Hospital," the doctor said, introducing himself as he tucked the clipboard under his arm. “A week ago, you came in here suffering from gunshot wounds to your chest and neck.” Vanessa looked at the him with wide eyes. “So, do you understand what I’m explaining to you?” Vanessa nodded her head up and down, the heart monitor now beeping louder and faster.

“Just calm down. You are going to be fine,” he said, patting Vanessa’s arm. “You have a lot to be thankful for. One is the night you got shot, you were wearing this.” He reached in the drawer next to the bed and revealed a chain with a diamond Jesus piece. “If the bullet that struck you in the chest didn’t come in contact with this chain first, there’s no doubt in my mind that you wouldn’t be here with us.”

Vanessa listened in horror as she patted her chest with trembling hands. She could feel the draining tube in her chest. She reached out and retrieved the jewelry from his hand. She turned the jewelry over in her shaky hand, assessing the damage jewelry. It clear where it had been struck as there was chunk missing from its face.

The memory switch turned on in her head and the tragic events came flooding back like a white water tide. She remembered arguing with Rob and flashes from a gun interrupting their disagreement. Vanessa couldn’t quite figure out what happened next or why she and Rob were arguing. She did, however, remember she took the chain out of BJ’s safe.

“Rob!” Vanessa forced herself to say in a raspy voice.

“Mr. Pulley was shoot also, but he’s on another floor recovering,” Dr. Edelman advised her.

“See him?” Vanessa said, licking her dry lips. Dr. Edelman looked at Nurse Gomez.

“Um, I don’t think that would be a good idea right now, but Mr. Pulley is doing fine and he’s recovering from his injuries. You should, too.”

“No, I want to see him,” Vanessa said a little over a whisper.

“No, Ms. Jones. I cannot let you see him at this time,” Dr. Edelman insisted. Her thoughts went to Rob. She was wondering if he really was okay and why they were giving her little information on him. She needed to know if the love of her life, her baby's father, was all right.

The baby, Vanessa thought as her hands shot down to her stomach. She could feel the emptiness in her. She already knew she had lost the baby, but she had to ask the dreaded question.

"My baby?" she asked with pleading eyes. Dr. Edelman let out a sigh.

"I'm sorry, Ms. Jones. The trauma from being shot and from the seizure you had yesterday was too much for the fetus to take," he told her, patting her arm before he left the room.

Vanessa's heart shattered into a million pieces. Her eyes began to release tears over the loss of her unborn child. She couldn't understand how God could be so caring in sparing her life but so cruel by taking her unborn child life. A mustard seed of hate began to grow inside her towards Rob. She instantly reached the conclusion she lost her child because of the life that Rob was living in the streets. She knew that whoever shot her was there to kill Rob, not her. She was at the wrong place at an unfortunate time. Vanessa cried even harder.

"Oh poor, Ms. Jones," Nurse Gomez said, leaning over and hugging her. Vanessa held on tightly to the friendly nurse. She didn't know her, but her opened arms were something that she needed. "It's going to be okay, girl. It's going to be just fine."

***

Homicide Jack and Channtel sat chit-chatting in his black Buick downtown on Chestnut Avenue. He watched his mirrors as he waited for LJ. "I can't wait until I'm able to move around like I want to, Chann. I know you're tired of driving me around and waiting on a nigga hand and foot," he said as he took a pull from his cancer stick.

"Baby, I wouldn't have it any other way What I have learned in the past is that 'what one woman won't do, another one will' and I'll be damned if I'm going to let another bitch come and take mines because I'm not doing my job," Channtel said with a little feistiness.

Their bond had grown over the past few months. They were inseparable unless Channtel had to go to work at the bar or if he had to go handle some business with BJ. But since he'd been shot, he'd been on ice, allowing and him and Channtel's relationship to grow even stronger.

"Naw, Chann. You know I would never let another woman come between us," he stated, looking at his Queen.

"It's not that I don't trust you, Homicide. It's them nasty ass bitches I don't trust," she said, balling her face up. "Here comes your boy," she told him, tapping him on the thigh as LJ was came up on the passenger's side. He got in the car, sliding his body to the middle of the back seat.

"What's good, playa? What's the urgent matter you had to see me about?" LJ asked.

Homicide Jack turned in his seat and faced him, shaking his head. "You fucked up bad, nigga," he said with disgrace in his voice.

"What? What the fuck done happened now?" he inquired.

"The 40 situation. That shit is not done!"

"Man, Homicide. Miss me with that shit. I took care of my business," he said, scanning the downtown scenery as he started to feel uneasy.

"Listen, nigga. That shit is not handled. 40 is still alive and he's at the Riverside Hospital and the broad you so happily gunned down was none other than BJ's sister!" he roared. LJ's forehead broke out into sweat after the bomb Homicide Jack just dropped on his lap.

"How the fuck I was supposed to know who the bitch was and what the hell was she doing with 40 anyway?" LJ questioned. Homicide Jack looked at LJ crazy for calling his boss's sister a bitch.

"Somehow, they got connected together, but you need to make some shit happen. BJ is asking for your head on this one. So, handle this hit. Then you can get back on his good side, allowing you to sit down at the table with the family," he instructed him. LJ nodded his head up and down.

"A'ight, you say that he's at the Riverside Hospital."

"Yeah, room five thirty on the fifth floor, but we already devised a plan to deal with 40. We got a inside source that's going to keep tabs on him until he gets released. When that time comes, we're going to be there and follow him home, pushing his shit back on his doorstep," he told him, looking around to make sure no one was paying the Buick and its occupants any attention.

"So, if you got it all figured out, why am I here?" LJ asked.

"Nigga you're the gun on his shit!" Homicide Jack snapped. "You the reason why we're here now. You missed your target twice and you fucked around and shot the contractor's sister after your ass got paid for it. So, your ass is here to handle the business you got paid for or you can hand me back the twenty-five grand I paid you." Homicide was furious, spit sprinkling from his mouth every time he raised his voice at LJ. Channtel and LJ's eyes met in the rearview mirror. LJ hated more than anything to be scorned in front of a woman, but he held his tongue.

"Aye, Homicide. I get where you're coming from. Just know that I'm on it. Provide me with the intel, that's all. When is he scheduled to be discharged from the hospital?"

"We don't know right now but when I find out, I will let you know."

"Well, when he does, I'ma be there to rock his ass to sleep," LJ spoke in a sinister like voice. Homicide nodded his head up and down as rubbed his goatee.

"I'm gone," LJ said, getting out the car and walking down Chestnut Avenue. He was livid that Homicide Jack talked to like that in front of Channtel. He knew he had to make a power move to get back in his good graces. Then he could get to BJ to fulfill the contract Fever had placed on his life.

LJ was hoping when Homicide Jack called, it was to set up a meeting with BJ. He would have made that hit right then and there on the spot. LJ patted the compact 9-millimeter and silencer he had on his hip. He met with Fever the other morning at IHOP where he gave him the one hundred thousand dollars in cash and run down on BJ.

LJ rubbed his hands together thinking about the money he had stashed at his two-bedroom apartment. Once he killed BJ, he would kill Homicide Jack for disrespecting him. But for now, he had a plan of his own.

Chapter 10

"What the fuck this nigga got going on," Toflon said to himself. He had just pulled up on the small block out in York Country off Durby Run. There was a crowd of niggas standing around in a circle. Toflon could see Fever standing there giving a speech. He wondered why he had summoned him too. Toflon checked his 45 Ruger, making sure one bullet was secured in the chamber before he placed the gun on his hip.

Toflon checked his surroundings once more before he exited his Acura. He inadvertently made his way over to the crowd with caution. When he got close enough, he could see Fever had a young kid on his knees with his right-hand man Bear standing over the kid, pointing a 44 Magnum to the back of the kid's head.

The men that stood around acted as if it this was the daily function on the block. Fever made eye contact with Toflon as he spoke. "Yo, don't I take care of my niggas?" he asked him in anger.

"Yup!" The circle of men chimed in together.

"Don't I make sure you nigga' eat good?" Fever asked.

"Yup!" all Fever flunkies said at once.

"Then why did this ungrateful little muthafucka steal from me?" he yelled. The kid looked terrified, his whole body shaking like a leaf on a tree on a windy night. "Ray-Ray, lay flat on the ground and extend your arms out to your side," he ordered.

Ray-Ray hesitated but after Bear nudged him in the head with the barrel of the 44, he came into compliance and followed Fever orders. He lied down on the concrete and extended his arms. The crowd of men looked on in amusement. Fever drew a work hammer from the small of his back. Bear placed his size 14 Timberlands on Ray-Ray's wrist, locking his arms into place.

"Ray-Ray, you are new in the game, so I'm not going to kill you. I am, however, going to teach you a hard lesson that's priceless. That lesson is you never bite the hand that feeds you!" Fever drew the hammer back in the air and brought it down, crashing Ray-Ray's hand that was held captive under Bear's foot.

"Aggghhhhhhh!" Ray-Ray cried out in pain, squirming on the concrete. He still couldn't get his pent hand wrist free from under Bear's boot. Ray-Ray cried out in agony only exciting Fever's sick twisted mind to cause more pain to the16-year-old's hand. Fever drew the hammer back a little further back then the last time. He then brought the it down on Ray-Ray's hand for the second time with so much force, a piece of bone fragment popped out, making contact with Toflon's black Air Force One's.

Ray-Ray went crazy as the excruciating pain exploded in his hand. "Agggghhh! Aghhhhh! Agghhh!" he yelled out, snot shooting from his nose as he cried out. Fever stood over Ray-Ray with a smirk on his face, his chest rising and falling rapidly. He enjoyed inflicting pain on others. Bear removed his foot from Ray-Ray's wrist. He drew up in a ball and cradled his hand.

"Let this be a lesson to you, Ray-Ray. Never bite the hand that feeds you," he said once more, handing Bear the work hammer.

Fever nodded his head at Toflon, motioning him to follow him. Fever led the way to a white brimstone house that sat in the middle of the block. Bear and three other dudes followed them into the house. Once Toflon was in, he could tell it was strictly for business only as it was barely furnished.

There was a couch sitting against the wall on the far-right side of the house and a round wooden table with four matching chairs. The most expensive item in the house was the 60-inch flat screen television that hung on the wall across from the couch. Fever took a seat at the table along with his goons. Bear took a standing position with Fever to his right while Toflon was to Fever's right.

"This the business shit going down tomorrow. We're riding out to Smithfield in the country. We're breaking up into two teams," Fever said, pulling out a drawn map. "Bear, you, Chief and Duke are going to be together. Me, Toflon, and Rocks are going to be together. There's an old farmhouse and a barn. A truck arrives with the four hundred pounds where they break the load down into two vans before transporting the weed into the city. Our job is to hit them while they are loading up the vans. We catch them by surprise and hit everything out that bitch. We get the weed and he head back to Bad News. We're heading out there around nine. I expect everyone here by seven thirty. If you're late, then you're hit. Any questions?" Fever asked.

"Yeah," Rocks said. "So, you just want us to go in with guns blazing?"

"If a fly moves out that bitch, I want it murdered," he informed his young soldier. "Are there any more questions? If not, then this meeting is over. Yo, Toflon. Let me holla at you," he said, pulling him away from the rest of the crew as they went into the kitchen.

It was small but clean. You could smell a light scent of weed in the air. Fever opened the refrigerator and grabbed two beers, handing one to Toflon. "What's good with that nigga BJ?" he asked, getting straight to the point as he took a swig from his beer.

"Fever, nothing came back on his whereabouts yet. Before all this shit happened, I didn't have a chance to get a good line on him," Toflon stated.

"Tell me again why BJ killed my brother?"

Toflon took a long drink from his beer. He wanted to get his story together. "Well, Butta, Pookie and me hit some niggas out in Hampton that was draggin' BJ about some money they owed him. So, BJ put us on the move to handle the situation." Toflon paused, taking another sip of beer before continuing. "Once we took care of our end of the deal, BJ didn't want to pay up. When we went to go holla at him about our money, he and his people just opened fire on us." Toflon lied with a straight face, but he could see a hint of betrayal in his eyes. He stared at Toflon without batting an eye.

"We got to get this nigga Toflon and I want to talk to Pookie too," he told him, displaying anger on his face.

"We'll find him, Fever. We'll find him," Toflon said, trying to reassure him.

***

"How's everything looking with the product?" Moe-B asked.

"Shit looking good with that, Moe-B," Mann stated. He was one of BJ's workers that Homicide Jack hired a few months ago. Mann was loyal to Homicide Jack, but he was also the type that was only tough when he was around his crew. If you caught him by himself, he was a straight bitch. Since he was older then Moe-B, Moe-B knew he was soft, chumping him every chance he got. "When Homicide Jack coming through?"

"Man, why the fuck you worried about my uncle for? You need to worry about getting that damn money together," Moe-B said, scolding Mann.

"I was just checking in on my boss."

"Your boss! I'm your fucking boss! I bring you the work." Moe-B raised the front of his shirt up, exposing the .357 that rested on his waistline.

"Yeah," Mann said nervously.

"You pay me for the product that I drop off, right?" Moe-B continued to interrogate Mann.

"Yeah!" Mann said, feeling disrespected but was to scared to say anything about it.

"Well then, nigga. I'm your boss. Now get the fuck to work," Moe-B said, laughing at Mann's bitch ass as he walked away like the sucker he was.

Moe-B threw the book bag strap over his shoulder and walked over to his cocaine white Charger. He was a slim dude with light brown curly hair that gave him that black Rico Suave look. He carried his 157 pounds with grace, standing 5' 7" with brown eyes that matched his brown-skinned complexion.

Moe-B loved to dress in the latest fashion. He prided himself on looking good at all times. Moe- B hopped in the Charger and pulled out. He was still feeling a certain type of way about how he was ordered to kill his cousin Lil Tate. He just didn't know how to approach Homicide Jack about it.

After the stunt BJ pulled the other day at Homicide Jack's apartment, Moe-B now viewed him in a different light and that situation alone added fumes to the flames. He felt his uncle killed his own flesh and blood for less, but didn't kill BJ even though his transgression was greater.

Moe-B didn't know what BJ had over his uncle, but it must be big because any other person who did that would have been a dead man right now. He shook his head thinking about it.at the thought. He knew he needed to holla at his uncle to see where his head was at before he made his move

Chapter 11

"Hey, Beautiful!" BJ said as he stepped into Vanessa's room holding a dozen of roses with Tashia following behind him. Vanessa tried to smile but it was weak.

"Hey, bruh," she stated dryly. She was still going through the emotional ride of losing her unborn child. BJ laid the flowers in her lap while Tashia hugged her.

"Hey, girl," Tashia said, holding on to Vanessa. They had become close like sisters.

"Hey, Tashia."

"You alright?" BJ asked, Tashia nodded her head up and down without saying a word. "Nessa, I thought I lost your ass," he said, planting a kiss on his sister's forehead. Vanessa's eyes watered over.

"It should have been me that died," she stated as a tear cascaded down her face.

"Why would you say that?" BJ inquired, looking confused.

"I should have died with my baby. I shouldn't be here," she said, her voice cracking.

"Vanessa, I understand where you are coming from but don't say shit like that. I need you, Nessa. If you die then I die. You all I got sis," BJ said, placing his hand out and grabbing Vanessa hand. His hand was met by something solid. BJ opened her hand a saw the disfigured Jesus piece in her hand. For the second time today, BJ look confused because the jewelry looked familiar. "What's this, sis?" BJ asked.

Vanessa stayed silent while looking down at the Jesus piece that rested in her hand. "This is the chain that saved my life the night I was shot. I was wearing this chain and the bullet that hit me in the chest lost it momentum because it hit the chain first. Dr. Edelman told me if this didn't happen then the bullet to the chest would have killed me for sure," Vanessa said, handing BJ the chain. Tashia just stood there in awe.

"This chain looks familiar," he stated, examining the chain.

"I took it from your safe." Vanessa dropped her head. BJ stared at her. He was furious, but he didn't want her to stress over it due to her current situation.

"It's okay, sis. It's no big deal. The chain was meant for you anyway," BJ said.

"Is that right?" Vanessa raised the head and look at her brother.

"Yeah, because if you weren't wearing it, you would have died. You said it yourself. So, it was meant for you," BJ said and Vanessa gave a slight smile.

"Hello, everyone!" Moocha said, walking into Vanessa's room.

Immediately, Tashia size her up. Tashia wasn't a slouch bitch by far, but Moocha had set her in defense mode for some reason.

"Hey, Nurse Gomez," BJ said.

"Now, I told you about that Nurse Gomez stuff. It's Moocha." Moocha pointed a finger at BJ smiling.

"Okay, my bad," he replied, putting his hand up in submission.

"Uh hum," Tashia said, clearing her throat. BJ caught on.

"Oh, Moocha. This is Tashia, my Queen," BJ said, smiling as he put it on the table that he was taken.

"Oh, how are you doing?" Moocha asked extending her hand to a stoned-face Tashia. She lightly gripped Moocha's fingertips and then lightly shook them, making her feel as though her didn't really want to shake her hand. *This bitch is shady,* Moocha thought to herself.

"I'm fine," Tashia replied, letting Moocha's hand go.

"Has she been taking care of you?" BJ asked, directing his question to Vanessa.

"Yeah, she I s that best nurse I ever had. She brings me extra Jello," Vanessa said, bringing the room into laughter.

"I told you I was going to do my best to take care of her," Moocha replied, walking over to Vanessa to check her drainage bag and placing a fresh bandage on her neck. Tashia then reached into her Channel's purse and removed a comb and brush, gently combing Vanessa hair.

"Vanessa, I'm not getting married until you are up and out this hospital." Tashia put this statement out there more so to let Moocha know she was sitting on the throne next to the King.

"Thank you! Tashia, that means a lot to me," she said.

"Yo, Moocha. I need to holla at you," he said, walking out into the hallway for some privacy. Tashia watched the two interact with one another from Vanessa's bedside. "I really need your help with something," he said as he looked around to see if anybody was within an earshot.

"Okay, what is it?" she asked

BJ hesitated. "I need to know when the nigga Robert Pulley will be discharge fro the hospital."

"Why would you want to know that?" she questioned in a hushed tone.

BJ stuck his hands in the pockets of his jeans and began to tell his lie.

"Well, I don't want my sister around Robert. It's obvious that someone wants him dead and when he gets out of here, I want Vanessa long gone away from here and him." Moocha just listened and watched BJ's lips as the lie just rolled right off of them.

"You must think I was born yesterday papi," Moocha said, rolling her neck. "I'm from Harlem and I know game when I see it and hear it. So, tell me the truth," she said, placing her manicured hands on her hips. BJ stared into her eyes for a sign that he could trust her, but Moocha just shook her head. "Naw, BJ. I don't want to know, just make sure you look out for me real good on this one."

BJ had beef with 40 and the way he was looking all around was a dead giveaway that he had something in store for Robert Pulley. After the incident he had two days ago with Rob, and how he demanded the hospital place Vanessa on a different floor, let Moocha see that their beef was serious.

"Look, the least you know, the better. But I will pay you a handsome fee for your help," he told her. She just nodded her head up and down in agreement. "You got to keep this under your hat. Vanessa don't need to know nothing about this," he whispered.

"Alight, BJ. My mouth is closed."

"Okay, that's what I'm talking about," he replied, sticking a fist out and letting Moocha's small fist give him a pound.

They both then walked back into Vanessa's room. BJ caught Tashia's eyes burning a hole in him. He wondered what got her all up tight. He walked over to Vanessa's bed. She had her eyes closed. The meds she was on had her sleeping peacefully with the Jesus piece in the palm in her hand. He removed it and planted a kiss on her cheek before he exited the room, leaving Tashia there to hold her hand. Moocha and Tashia made eye contact, Tashia shooting daggers at her.

"Girl, don't no one want your man," Moocha said under her breath as she made an exit to make her rounds.

Chapter 12

The janitor eased his supply cart down the hallway of Riverside Hospital. He whistled taking in his surroundings as he made his way down the corridor of the fifth floor. Every few feet, he would mop a spot on the floor with a damp mop, then place a wet mop sign where he had mopped.

The gray janitor jumper fitted LJ nicely. He found a janitor closet earlier that day where he been hiding for the last five hours. LJ made it in the hospital without any detection, so he didn't want to be notice by hospital staff, hiding in the janitor closet until the right time and opportunity presented itself.

LJ was a very patient man, which made him good at what he did. That was being a contract killer. He was on a mission to finish the job on 40. There was no way he was going to wait until 40 was discharged from the hospital. He had every intention to end this shit now while 40 was weak and vulnerable.

LJ knew this move came with risks, but he had been a risk taker all of his life. Once this was done, he could ease back into Homicide Jack's good graces, meet BJ, then cash in on the contract that Fever had placed on BJ's head. He placed another wet floor sign down as he continued whistling and making his way down the hall towards 40' s room.

***

40 sat in his hospital bed with a note pad and a ballpoint pen resting on his lap. He was trying to formulate his thoughts and write Vanessa a letter. He was livid BJ's bitch ass had her moved to another floor. Nurse Gibblings refused to tell him which floor she was on, but she did give him the idea to write letter. If he did, she agreed to deliver it to her on his behalf.

Throughout the whole ordeal that took place with them in Vaneessa's room, no one even questioned how 40 got to her room in a wheelchair with a broken arm.

40's eyes became heavy as the pain medication he took earlier was strong, forcing him to sleep. He closed his eyes and his thoughts begun to drift to Vanessa's beautiful face. He would have given anything to touch her face right now. 40 drifted into a slumber.

***

LJ mopped in front of 40's room and placed a wet floor sign in front of the door. He looked around one last time before he made his way in the room. He eased over to the machine that was monitoring 40's vitals and softly killed the power switch. The switch made a light click sound, but do to the dead silence of the hospital, the click as if someone had snapped their fingers.

LJ watched 40's chest rise and fall. He knew that he didn't have much time. He fished some rope out his pocket and wrapped it tightly around both of his hands. He then slid the middle part of the rope around his neck, awakening him from his sleep. 40's eyes shot open as he fought for air. The fight was easily won by his capturer's rope around his neck. Due to him only having one usable arm, he didn't have a fighting chance. 40 kicked and tried to yell, but the wires that held his jaws shut wouldn't allow him to. he tried to get a finger in between his neck and the rope, but the rope was too tight.

"This is from BJ, bitch ass nigga," LJ whispered in 40' s ear, pulling tighter on the rope. This made him fight harder, but it still wasn't no use. He could feel his lungs burning from the lack of air. The harder he fought, the harder LJ pulled back on the rope. Snot started to bubble out of 40's nose, his blood vessels erupting in his eyes causing blood to seep from them.

His body begun to twitch and jerk as his world became dark. All he could do was think about Vanessa and him not being able tell her he was sorry. His body laid still as LJ loosened the rope from around his neck. He stood over 40 for a brief second breathing heavily. He placed the covers back over his body and made it appear that he was sleeping. Smiling to himself, LJ double checked to make sure that he left nothing behind. Feeling satisfied, he made his way back into the hallway and continued to mop his way back down the hallway from the way he came from.

***

"You ready to get this paper, nigga?" Fever asked Toflon and Rocks. They both nodded their heads up and down. Bear and his team had already passed the farmhouse, making their way towards the barn. They barely could be seen draped in their all black attire. Smithfield Country was quiet. All you could hear were the crickets and the mosquitos was biting and holding. A delivery truck had just pulled into the barn fifteen minutes earlier. Fever was waiting for them to break the load down into the two separate vans before he made his entrance. "Bear!" Fever whispered into his headset.

"Yeah, boss?" Bear's voice barked loudly through the headset.

"You move in on my word."

"Gotcha!" Bear agreed.

The high-grade marijuana came all the way from Cali. This was the final stop before it was brought into Newport News. Fever learned this from his ex-business partner Aymir until he crossed him out on a thousand-pound deal. Fever and his team revealed themselves after hiding behind a John Dear tracker. They started to make their way to the back entrance of the barn. Toflon, starting to get a bad feeling, hung back just a second as he looked towards the farmhouse. He saw the door curtains move.

Bear and his team had just barely made it to the front of the barn. They were fifty yards out when the farmhouse's door opened. A blond head chick stepped out onto the porch, carrying an Uzi followed by two big bullmastiffs. "Get 'em," the woman ordered the dogs.

The trained beasts went into attack mode, charging towards Bear and his team like two raging bulls. They took cover behind a fallen oak tree that was between them and the farmhouse. The sound of the dogs alerted Aymir's men who were unloading the delivery truck. Fever's gun bucked hard in his hand.

Boom!

The sound caused the farm's nightlife to go into a full-fledged gun battle. The 45 slug pushed Aymir's worker's head back to unrecognizable figure. Fever kept firing his gun as the men in the barn defended their boss's product.

Boom! Boom! Boom! Bong! Bong! Bong!

The men traded gunfire, Rock getting struck in the stomach. Fever looked over his shoulder and saw Toflon was nowhere in sight. "Bitch ass nigga," he mumbled as he returned fire at the woman on the porch of the farmhouse. The Uzi she was spraying was giving him hell.

Tat! Tat! Tat! Tat! Tat! Tat! Tat! Tat!

It was like the bitch never ran out of bullets. She kept shooting and the bullets kept coming. One of the bullmastiffs reached Bear, grabbing a hold of his shoulder and locking on. Bear hollered liked a bitch as the dog's teeth tore into his flesh, but Bear didn't have bitch in him. He rolled over on top of the dog while still ducking the wrath of the woman's Uzi. He forced the muzzle of his 44 under the dog's jawbone and squeezed the trigger.

Boom!

The gun roared. The bullets tore through the dog's skull, knocking half of its face off and painting Bear's face with dog matter as blood prematurely blinded him. Duck dropped the other dog before it had a chance to get to him. Toflon used the darkness to shield his presence as he raced to the side of the farmhouse where the woman was reloading the Uzi. She was slamming a fresh clip into the gun when she heard, "Pssst." When she turned around, she was met with two dome shots by Toflon's 19.

Blocka! Blocka!

Toflon picked the Uzi up and stepped over the woman's dead body as he sprinted towards the barn. Chief laid out dead next to one of the bullmastiffs that Bear had killed. Chief had three large holes in his chest.

Fever entered the barn catching one of Aymir's men trying to hide behind the large barn door. "Get your bitch ass out here," Fever ordered The man coming out of hiding, pointed his gun at him. The man eased out from behind the barn's door. He clutched an empty Desert Eagle. If he had one more bullet left, he would have taken his last shot at Fever.

"Listen, just take the weed and leave," the man said.

The rest of Fever's men came into the barn and began emptying the delivery truck and loading the two vans with the weed. "Man, you don't have to do this," the captured man stated.

"Did I tell your ass to speak? Huh, bitch?" Fever screamed, his anger silencing the man. "Get them vans loaded!" he ordered Bear and Duck. "Tim, now you feel how it feels to be shit ted on. Aymir didn't have to cut me out that deal. All he had to do was keep the business straight and everything would have been good."

"But I have nothing to do with that, Fever. I'm just a worker," Tim complained.

"You have everything to do with this. You're part of the opposing team," Fever replied. Tim couldn't say anything. Fever made note that Toflon wasn't in the barn. He hoped he was dead. If not, Toflon was going to wish that he was dead for leaving him in the midst of a gun battle. Then out of nowhere, a figure rolled from under one van and placed a .357 to the back of Fever's head, cocking it hammer back. "Drop the gun, you piece of shit."

Automatically, Fever's hands flew to the air. He gritted his teeth in frustration, letting the gun fall from his hands. He knew he was fucked.

The capturer picked Fever's gun up. Him and Fever never liked each other, Fever starring down his famous .357 he always carried which was troubling to him. Bear and Duck caught off guard, stopped loading the vans as they, put their hands in the air. "Drop your guns!" Paulie ordered Bear and Duck, still holding his gun to Fever head. They both came into compliance. The once frightened Tim got up of the gun and retrieved Fever's gun from Paulie.

"Get the fuck on your knees!" Tim commanded Fever, pointing the gun in his face.

"Naw, bitch. You got me fucked up. If you're going to kill me, do me standing on my ten toes. I don't kneel to no man," Fever said, showing no fear.

Tim slapped him with the gun and pulled the trigger at the same time. The 45 roared.

Boom!

The gun sent a deafening roar into Fever's ear, bringing him to his hands and knees effortlessly. His ears rung in pain and water filled his eyes. For once in Fever's life, he felt fear. He knew tonight he was going to die. He could feel it in the air. Bear and Duck watched in horror as Fever's soon-to-be executioner stood over him clutching a now smoking 45. Paulie held Bear and Duck at bay with his 357.

"You still want to die standing on you ten toes, nigga?" Tim said in his Arab accent. Tim pointed the gun at Fever's head. He applied a little pressure on the trigger. Fever closed his eyes.

Blocka! Blocka!

Tim's head exploded, spraying Fever's face with blood. Paulie turned around and opened up his big Cannon.

Boom! Boom!

He back peddled out the barn.

Blocka!

He caught a bullet to the shoulder that made him drop his gun and sprint out the barn. Toflon pursued him banging his gun.

Blocka! Blocka! Blocka!

Paulie went about fifty yards before a bullet slammed into his butt cheek. Paulie dropped to the ground and played dead. Toflon stood in the doorway of the barn as he watched Paulie drop and lay still. He was satisfied that he was dead. Toflon helped Fever to his feet. Fever's ears were still ringing as he tried to shake the pain from them. Toflon went with Bear and Duck to help them finish unloading the vans.

Fever saw Toflon in a different light after the incident. The thought of having him killed was starting to fade. Fever searched Tim's pockets for the keys to the vans. He tossed Bear a set of keys. Bear and Duck got in one of the van while Toflon rode shotgun with Fever.

Toflon was already thinking about the hundred grand he would receive for his assistance. He didn't even know he had just secured his life tonight.

****

Lying in the damp grass fifty yards away from the barn, Paulie heard the vans leaving. He struggled to get his phone out his pocket. The bullet in his ass really started to burn. He hit his boss on speed dial and the phone was answered on the first ring.

"Hello."

"Aymir, we got a problem. We've been robbed."

Chapter 13

"I don't care what you say, BJ. I'm not feeling Nurse Gomez or Moocha, whatever the bitch name is," Tashia said with much attitude, while snaking her neck from side to side.

"Come on, Tashia. Where are all these insecurities coming from all of sudden?" BJ asked, taking a sip of his apple juice.

"Insecurities? Boy, you got me twisted. I can't believe you even said some shit like that out your mouth. That bitch has nothing to make me feel insecure about. I just know a shiesty bitch when I see one.' Tashia took another bite of her French vanilla pancakes.

"And that's what I'm saying it, Tashia. Moocha has nothing on you, love." BJ was stroking his woman ego. He knew Moocha gave Tashia a run for her money on any given day, but he would never admit that though. "And how shady could the girl be, Tashia? She works at a hospital, not a strip club."

"What difference does it make where she works at? You got all type of shady muthafuckas working everywhere," she fussed, raising her voice a little too loud, bringing attention their way as the occupants in IHOP glared their way.

"Come on, Tashia. Keep your voice down."

"Listen, all I'm saying is don't trust the bitch. I'm getting a bad feeling about her," Tashia stated firmly, scooping a fork full of eggs in her mouth.

"And you got all of that from your first encounter with her?" BJ questioned.

"You muthafuckin' right!" Tashia shot back. BJ just shook his head. "Baby, never forget this. It only takes only bullet to kill you, one slip up to send you to jail for life. Just because I only met her once doesn't mean my instincts are inaccurate," Tashia said, dropping a jewel on BJ. Now she had BJ thinking

"Alright, I'm gonna take heed to what you are saying, Tashia. I will not trust her until I get a better read on her," he replied, pushing his plate to the side and checking his phone.

"Damn, Tashia. I thought that was you over here looking all good," some guy said, walking up to their table.

"Oh hey, Wallo!" Tashia said which brought BJ's eyes up from his phone to meet Wallo's eyes, eye fucking her as if he wasn't even there in the restaurant.

"Ain't too much. Just saw you over here and wanted to know if you've heard about 40. That shit is all over the news," Wallo said. BJ's ears perked up and Tashia began to stumble with her words.

"No—No, what happened to 40?" she asked.

"Man, someone went in the Riverside Hospital last night and murked ole boy in his room." Tashia's mouth dropped open.

"Oh my God! Damn, Wallo. I haven't heard that."

"Yeah, that shit all over the news. The Riverside Hospital is on straight lock down. Nothing's going in or out that bitch right now, according to the news anyway." BJ and Tashia briefly made eye contact.

"Damn, that's crazy, Wallo. First it was Block, then it was Skalez and now it's 40," she said, playing her role to the fullest.

"So, is this your man?" Wallo asked.

"Oh yeah. This my man, BJ." Wallo for a second, balled his face up, but immediately held his composure. "Baby, this Wallo. Wallo this is BJ," Tashia said, introducing the two.

"Nice to meet you," Wallo replied, sticking his fist out to BJ for a pound. BJ hit Wallo's fist.

"What's up, fam?" BJ made eye contact with Wallo who stood there stone-faced.

"Ain't too much, playboy. I think I heard your name ringing throughout Newport News. You be on twenty-fourth street, right?" Wallo asked. This line of questioning caught BJ off guard and Wallo peeped it in his body language.

"Naw, fam. Wrong BJ," he replied. For a moment, a brief silence fell around the table.

"Well, let me leave you two love birds to your brunch," Wallo said, turning on his heels, but before he took a step, he turned back around. "Oh, before I go. Tashia, have you heard anything about my cousin Skalez's murder? BJ's hand dropped to his waist hearing Skalez's name.

"No, Wallo. I haven't heard shit about that," she said, lying through her teeth without even batting an eye.

"A'ight, I'm gone," he told her, walking away from their table. Their eyes burned hole into Wallo's back from watching him too hard.

"Damn, Tashia! What the fuck!" BJ said, shaking his head to left to right. "You think he knows I had something to do with killing Skalez?"

"I don't think so. Baby," she replied, trying to calm her nerves.

"But in the event that he does, I'm going to need all the info you have on him," BJ said, dialing a number on his phone.

"Hello," Homicide Jack, said answering the phone on the third ring.

"Yo, Homicide. This BJ. I need to holla at you about some serious shit." Homicide Jack could hear the seriousness in BJ's voice.

"Okay, I'll slide past your crib in about a hour," he said, disconnecting the call. BJ placed another call. Once the person on the other end of the phone answered, BJ went to talking. "Yo, Moocha. This is BJ." BJ's eyes went to Tashia who sat across the table from him. She threw her hands in the air and mouthed the words "what the fuck". BJ ignored her gesture. "What's good? How is Vanessa?"

Moocha's voice went into a whisper. "Vanessa is fine, but you better not bring your ass to his hospital to see her," Moocha said.

"What? Why would you say that?" BJ was trying to play the dumb role as he tried to get information out of Moocha that he possibly couldn't know.

"Nigga, you think you got all the sense. You know exactly why you better not come past the hospital."

"Moocha, what the fuck you talking about?" BJ asked her, still sticking to his guns about not knowing what was going on.

"BJ, somebody killed Robert Pulley last night. The police want to talk to you about the altercation you had with him at the hospital."

"What? Fuck!" BJ's heart begun to race a million beats a minute. His eyes met Tashia's. All she could see was panic in his eyes. "A'ight, Moocha. Let me hit my lawyer up and I'll get back with you. Just make sure Vanessa is a'ight. Just get back with me if you hear anything."

"Ok, BJ. I will," she replied. BJ hit the end button on the phone, then placed it on the table, shaking his head in frustration.

"Baby, what's going on?" Tashia asked with concern in her voice.

"It's true that 40 was murdered last night, but the crazy part is the police are looking for me. They want me to come for questioning." Tashia just listened in horror. She placed her hand over her mouth. "I'm going to go to the house to meet with Homicide and Bugg and run everything down to them. In the meantime, I need you to get on line and find the best criminal defense lawyer Newport News has to offer. We will pay him or her a retainer fee and I'll go in for questioning with the lawyer," he said, giving Tashia instructions.

"Okay, BJ. I'm on it!" she agreed, grabbing her phone out her Channel purse and searching the Internet.

BJ picked his phone up and called Bugg, his business partner, giving him the run down on the situation. He asked him to meet him at the crib in a hour. BJ disconnected the call, dropping a few bills on the table for the waitress. His mind was all over the place. He wondered who killed 40.

This shit just brought a brand-new type of heat his him. He knew it couldn't be LJ's doing because he'd already been given orders on how to deal with 40 once he was discharged from the hospital. BJ made his way out of IHOP with Tashia's eyes glued to her phone.

BJ's mind was so occupied with his current situation that he didn't even know he had a dangerous set of eyes on him.

Chapter 14

"Good morning, Vanessa. How are you feeling, mami?" Moocha asked as she walked into her room, closing the door.

"I'm feeling much better. Just can't wait to get out this damn hospital and get this nappy ass head of mines washed and get into some clothes."

"I definitely hear your cry to be pampered." Moocha smiled as she walked over to Vanessa's bedside to change the bandage on her neck. She checked the wound, which was healing gracefully. "If you want, I could wash your hair or you," Moocha suggested.

"Oh, no. I can't have you doing that. You've already been waiting on me hand and foot," she said. Vanessa and Moocha had been building a homegirl bond with one another. Moocha was her blanket of comfort during those times of hardship. Vanessa enjoyed the spunky nurse's company. She always called for Moocha to do something just to keep her in the room, like getting her extra crushed ice or Jello from the cafeteria.

"Are you sure, Vanessa? I really don't mind," Moocha asked.

"Yeah, I'm sure, but thank you though. Hey, why you got my door closed? It's been like that all morning," Vanessa said with concern. Moocha became nervous. She didn't want to lie, but also, she didn't want to be the one to burden her with bad news.

"Ummm, everyone's door is closed shut today. That's protocol when the hospital is placed on lockdown."

"Lockdown! What you mean lockdown? I thought lockdowns were only for prisons. Shit, I know I got to hurry up and get out of this hospital now," she said with a frown on her face.

Moocha chuckled. "Yeah, girl. This place is on lockdown status. Someone died on the fifth-floor last night and they—" Moocha said before she was interrupted by two mean looking detectives that had just walked into the room.

She saw them earlier talking to Dr. Edelman in the hallway. She overheard them asking about BJ and the altercation he had with 40. “Can I help you, gentlemen?” Moocha asked them, stepping forward and stopping the detectives.

“Yes, we are here to talk to Ms. Jones,” the leading detective stated who was oil slick black and pudgy in the midsection.

“First of all, if you want to speak to Ms. Jones, you need to knock on the door and wait to be acknowledged before entering. You just don’t barge into a room. This is hospital, not a police station. Please show some respect. I could have been in here giving her a bath,” Moocha scolded the two detectives. They were stunned that she was reading them the way that she was. After all, they were Newport News finest.

“Oh, we are so—sorry, ma’am!” the black detective said, stumbling with his words. The light brown skinned detective rolled his eyes at Moocha.

“Now that the respect has been established—” Moocha stated, turning around to Vanessa. “—Ms. Jones, do you wish to speak to these gentlemen?”

“Well, who are they and why do they want to speak with me?” she asked.

“My name is Andy Tillman and this here is my partner, Frank Thomas. We are homicide detectives for Newport News. We would like to ask you a few questions about Robert Pulley.”

Vanessa knew the drill from living in the hood. See no evil, hear no evil and definitely speak no evil. She surely wasn’t going to give up any information on him even though she somewhat blamed him for the death of their unborn child.

“Okay, what you want to know?” she asked.

“Well, before we get started—” Frank Thomas replied then stopped. “—Ms. Gomez, you’re going to have to leave the room,” he said with a grin on his face. Moocha rolled her eyes at the detective. She hated the police, but she could play the game if Detective Thomas wanted to play.

"Ms. Jones, I'll be back in twenty minutes for your morning bath."

Vanessa picked up the hint. She knew Moocha didn't come to give her bath until after 12.

"Okay, Nurse Gomez," Vanessa replied as she walked out the room, leaving her at the mercy of the detectives.

"Ms. Jones, what's the relationship between you and Robert Pulley?" Detective Tillman asked as his partner pulled out a small note pad from his pocket with a pen to take notes.

"Uummm, I'm his girlfriend," Vanessa stated.

"And how long have you two been together?"

"Well, about ten months now." Vanessa rubbed her cold hands together.

"It's my understanding that someone tried to kill you and Mr. Pulley." Detective Tillman made eye contact with her when he asked.

"Yeah, they tried."

"Who is they?" Detective Tillman asked sharply before the statement got completely out of her mouth. Her face was now balled her up.

"I don't know," she replied in frustration. Detective Tillman looked at Vanessa sternly.

"What about your brother, Bryant Jones?

"My brother? What does my brother have to do with me and Rob getting shot?" Vanessa was getting mad as they insinuated he could be the person that shot them.

"He has everything to do with it. Do you know that your brother came to his same hospital and attacked Mr. Pulley while he was outside you room in a wheelchair?"

"No, my brother wouldn't do that!" Vanessa's breathing became rigid.

"Do you know where we can find your brother, Ms. Jones?" Detective Tillman asked with malice in his voice.

"N—no!" Vanessa struggled to answer.

"Ms. Jones, do you know anyone who would come in this hospital and kill your boyfriend? He was murdered last night."

The machine resting next to her bed started going haywire, all types of alarms beeping. The detective looked confused. She grabbed her chest as she struggled to breath. The door to the room opened, a doctor and nurse rushing in along with Nurse Gomez.

"Sorry, sir. Could you please leave? We need the room. You two have caused enough damage for today," Moocha said, slamming the door behind them cursing under her breath.

Vanessa was having a panic attack. Her lungs tightened in her chest. The type of stress the detectives caused wasn't good for her current condition. A nurse placed an oxygen mask over her face, while Moocha rubbed her back, smoothing her out of her panic attack. "Come on, Ms. Jones. Just breathe. I got you. Just breathe," Moocha whispered.

Chapter 15

BJ put the Bic lighter's flame to the end of the neatly rolled backwood, pulling on the sour tasting cannibals until the cherry head settled on the end of it.

All that could be heard in the room was him pulling on the backwood as Homicide Jack and Bugg patiently waited for him to reveal why he had called this meeting. He inhaled deeply, letting the purp do what it does best for him, which was smooth him over and put him in a calm-like state. His eyes met Homicide's.

"Shit all bad, Homicide," BJ told him, taking another pull of the purp. Homicide Jack didn't say anything. He was waiting for BJ to speak on it. "Some stupid muthafucka went inside Riverside Hospital and murdered your boy 40 last night," he told him as he sat on the edge of the living room window seal.

Homicide Jack closed his eyes and shook his head. He knew this was straight up bad news. BJ hit the purp again and tapped the ashes in the ashtray that rested on the lip of the window seat beside him. "Did your people do this?" he asked him.

"I don't know, young blood. I gave him specific orders on how we were going to handle 40 once he got out the hospital. I'll find out though," he replied, rubbing his hand over his bald head.

"This shit didn't do nothing but put heat on me. The police want me for questioning about 40's murder. I'ma have to go in and talk to them."

"Fuck naw, nigga. Is you crazy? You going to walk right into the lion's den?" Bugg asked him.

"Fam, I'm going to walk in that bitch with my lawyer. I shouldn't have too much to worry about. I didn't do the hit on 40. Them facts they cannot change," BJ stated firmly.

"So, why they want to question you then?" Bugg asked.

"I'm a suspect because a few days ago I caught 40 coming outta Vanessa's room. My emotions got the best of me, so I punched him in his shit."

"Damn! BJ, you crazier than a muthafucka," Bugg said, laughing.

"Yeah, but this has placed me in a bad position. The police won't let me move like I want to throughout the city until they find out who killed him," he said, hitting the backwood a final time. He then walked over and handed the purp to Homicide Jack who sitting on the love seat.

Homicide Jack's phone rang. He was about to ignore it until he saw who it was. He motioned for BJ and Bugg to be quiet. "Yeah, speak on it," he said when he answered the phone.

"What good, Homicide Jack?" LJ asked.

"Shit, you tell me?" he said, shooting him a no-nonsense response.

"Well, turn the TV on to the news and that will tell you what's good," LJ stated with a hint of sarcasm in his voice.

"I done seen it. So, you're telling me that's your work?" Homicide Jack questioned. LJ didn't want to incriminate himself over the phone, but he answered him the best way he could.

"Does a bear have a furry ass?" LJ replied.

Homicide Jack let out a long sigh. "Pssssss. Nigga, you a fucking fool. I gave you orders to handle that shit a specific way and a specific time," he shot back, talking in codes as he spoke through clenched teeth.

"Homicide, what's the big deal? The shit was handled properly and no one saw the night hawk snatch the pigeon from the pigeon's coup," LJ talked back in codes, letting him know there were no eyewitnesses.

"Yeah, there's no one speaking on the evil, but damn, you put the boss under the magnifying glass of suspicion with them local boys," Homicide Jack told him, while holding eye contact with BJ.

BJ sat on the window ledge and listened intensely. LJ paused on the other end of the phone. He was at a loss for words.

"Um, how bad it the damage, Homicide Jack?" LJ asked

"Bad enough! But the damage has yet to be determined," Homicide Jack replied. "Look, I'm going to hit you up later when I find out something." LJ disconnected without a word. "Well, we know now our man did the job on 40," Homicide Jack said, passing the backwood to Bugg. He needed something stronger than some weed.

"Fuck!" BJ screamed out. "Okay, listen. I'm going to meet up with the lawyer and turn myself in, but in the event that they hold me, you two have to keep shit moving. Keep the trap house full. We got to open a new one to replace the trap house we lost on twenty-fourth. Homicide, that's your job. Bugg, you meet with the connect. Place an order for double on what we've been getting. I'm going to have Tashia hit you with my half of the money. I want a brick placed on Toflon's head. We have to move fast on this. We have to get back under the radar and get this money. All this murder is fucking up the business," BJ said.

"I agree, young blood. That's how it is when the streets clap back," Homicide Jack said.

"I'm on top of the connect. I'll hit him when I leave here," Bugg told him. His voice shook with a little concern.

"A'ight, then let me meet up with this lawyer." BJ stood up from sitting on the ledge of the window, giving them both a shoulder hug as he escorted them to the door.

***

20 minutes earlier

A black Dodge Magnum sat across the street from BJ's and Tashia's house. The occupant sat low in the driver's seat. The man intensely watched their residence like a pimp would watch his whore walk the whore stroll. The 30 round Ruger sat calmly on his lap, which gave him easy access to it if he needed. The driver watched his mirrors and paid close attention to his surroundings. The Hampton neighborhood was above middle class. All the houses on the block sat pretty with manicured lawns and expensive cars in the driveway.

BJ's back came into view in the window. From where the driver sat, he could see him smoking on something that appeared to be a blunt. He watched the dark white smoke seep from his nose. He could tell BJ was sitting in the window talking to someone by the way that he was moving his hands and head.

The driver realized killing him was going to be easy. He could easily put a bullet in the back of his head from where he sat. He picked the 30 shot Ruger up with a glove-covered hand. He turned his body in the seat and rolled the window down. He pointed the gun at the back of BJ's head as he sat in the window. The driver didn't want to point the gun out the window, so he leaned back in the driver's seat, placing BJ's head in his gun's sight.

He took a deep breath, trying to relax himself for the perfect shot. He placed his finger inside the trigger guard and on the trigger. He was now waiting for BJ to stop moving. Then his head came to a stop. The driver was ready to take the shot, applying some pressure on the trigger.

"Excuse me," a pizza delivery guy pulled up in a beat-up Honda, blocking the shooter's shot. "Oh shit!" he said when he saw the gun pointing his way. He immediately pushed down on the gas and the car exhilarated down the block.

"Shit!" the shooter said to himself, throwing the gun in the passenger's seat. He started up the Dodge Magnum and pulled off. He couldn't take a shot now and risk leaving any witnesses. Still, now he got a lead on him. So, he definitely knew he would have another chance.

Chapter 16

LJ hung up the phone confused. Everything about this hit had gone wrong or made shit more difficult for him to get close to BJ. He knew he was going to have to improvise, finding a way for BJ to be identified as 40's killer. He knew at this point, he had to be very careful because there was a possibility that Homicide Jack and BJ wanted him dead.

Shit, if he was in their shoes, he would want the same thing. LJ had a lot to think about. He needed to contemplate his next move and execute it ASAP. He took a sip of vodka from the Grey Goose bottle. "Agghhhh," he said as he sat the bottle down on the table, letting the clear liquor burn its way down his throat.

He picked up the keys to his 1500 RAM truck off the table. He needed to clear his mind and there was no better way than hitting up the hood and catching one of them young freaky bitches that was willing to do something strange for a little change with an old man.

***

Pookie pulled up in front of his baby mother's house. He checked his surroundings before he got out his car. He hadn't seen her or his daughter in a couple of weeks. He had to disappear for a hot minute after the shoot out on twenty-fourth street. The flesh wound he received bleed like hell, but once he got the bleeding to stop, it was all good.

Pookie had been watching the news. They reported that Lil Tate and Butta were pronounced dead at the scene. He didn't hear anything about Toflon and that concerned him. He felt bad about betraying Butta and Toflon for the thirty grand he got for setting them up, but he told himself, *Toflon shouldn't have killed BJ's mother. Some shit you just don't do or the streets will clap back.*

Brushing those thoughts aside, Pookie hoped he could get back in his baby mother Cely's good graces for abandoning her and his daughter for the last few weeks. He didn't come empty handed though. He came bearing gifts for Cely and his seven year-old-daughter, Layla.

Pookie was fresh to death stepping out his new whip, a Dodge Viper. His crisp all white Air Force Ones were spotless. The black Polo jeans he wore sagged slightly off his backside. The white and black Polo shirt fitted nicely. The Polo frames that rested on his face gave him a college look with a hint of street swagger.

Even though Pookie was paid a measly thirty racks for the double cross he laid down on his friends, it felt like he had a hundred thousand. Grabbing the bags out the back seat, he made his way inside Cely's apartment building. The hallway reeked with piss.

What muthafucka took a piss in the hallway, Pookie thought to himself. He made up his mind that he was going to move Cely and Layla out this dump. He stuck his key in the door and let himself in. The first thing he saw when he walked in was Layla. Her eyes landed on him. "Daddy!" she screamed, jumping and running to him as she abandoned her cartoon show to show him some love.

"Hey, my pretty Angel. How's daddy favorite little girl?"

"I'm good, daddy! Where you been, daddy?" Layla asked in her little kid's voice.

"Daddy been out buying you some things," Pookie said, telling half-truths. He reached in the bag and handed her a small pink box. She opened it and started jumping up and down.

"Oh, Daddy. They pretty!" Layla said, holding the box with two small pink diamond earrings in it. She was just like her mother, a diva.

"Layla, who are you talking to—" Cely stopped talking once her eyes landed on Pookie. She immediately balled her face up. "You need to go back to that bitch you was with!"

She snaked her neck and cocked her hip to the side, placing a hand on it. Cely was a pretty redbone who stood an even 5'8" and wore 145 pounds. She had more ass than she had breast, but no one ever complained about it thought.

She was one of those good girls that got lost in the hood of Newport News. She didn't have many sex partners, but a lot of men pursued her. She never really had anything in life, but that motivated her to keep up her appearance at all times, craving material things.

"Yo, Cely. Just hear me out!" Pookie said, trying to get a word in.

"Nigga, I ain't trying to hear shit you got to say." Cely said, cutting Pookie off.

"I know that shit looks fucked up, but some crazy shit happened."

"What happened that was so fucked up that you had to abandon your family?" she asked.

"Cely, I didn't abandon my family. Some shit just came up and I had to get ghost for a minute," Pookie explained, trying to plead his case. Layla hated when her parents fussed and fought. It made her sad. She ran to her room to get away from all the screaming.

"What came up that was so important, huh?" Cely replied as her eyes started watering. "Go ahead and lie like you always do," she said with misty eyes.

"It was this!" Pookie said, pulling ten grand out his pocket and tossing it to Cely. She caught the money in midair. She looked at the brick of money in her hand with three red rubber bands holding the money together. The money seemed foreign to her as if it didn't belong in her hands. She flipped through the tip of the bills and saw that there wasn't nothing but 100s and 50s.

"Where you get this, Pookie? Cely asked, still looking dumbfound at the money.

"Don't worry about where it came from. Just know I'm here to move you and our daughter out this fucking dump."

Cely rushed over to him and placed her arms around his neck. She passionately kissed his lips. She then pulled away from him with her arms still around his neck. "I got some good news. My cousin got me a job working at his paralegal firm. I'm just answering the phones and filing paper work, but it pays good money. So, with this money and the new job, we'll be okay if we just live inside our means of money. All we need to do is get you out them streets and get you a job," she said, looking into Pookie's eyes.

"That's great news, baby and I been thinking about getting out the streets. I'll give it a try for my family," he agreed, kissing Cely and grabbing a hand full of her ass. She sucked on his tongue hungrily. Pookie's manhood started to grow in his jeans as grinded against it. She pushed her hand down his jeans into his boxers and stroked him. He grew harder in her hand.

Knock! Knock! Knock!

The heard someone knocking at the door, stopping them from kissing and fondling. "Damn, who the fuck is this?" Pookie said, getting agitated that someone was cock blocking from getting his dick wet.

He went and snatched the door open without checking to see who it was. The blow to the bridge of Pookie's nose instantly brought him pain and blurry vision. He fell on his knees, grabbing his bleeding nose as blood gushed out between his fingers.

Toflon stepped in the apartment with a military edition 45, wearing a sinister smile. Cely froze in fear. Toflon closed the apartment door behind him and looked down at a frightened Pookie.

"What, you thought a nigga wasn't going to come for you?" asked Toflon. Pookie didn't say anything as he continued to hold his nose. He knew Toflon was going to kill him, so there was no need to speak and plead for his life. He knew the penalty for his betrayal was death.

"Please, Toflon. Don't hurt him. Pookie is your friend," Cely cried out.

Toflon didn't even look at her. He just pointed the 45 at her and pulled the trigger.

Boom!

The impact of the gun pushed the front of Cely's head out the back of her head, painting the wall behind her dark crimson red. The brain matter that splattered on the wall looked like Ramen noodles.

"No!" Pookie yelled out, crawling over to Cely's body that was jerking. "No! Not Cely!" Pookie loved his baby's mother. He cradled her in his arms, rocking her back and forth. Toflon knew gunshots would bring unwanted attention, so he had to act fast. He stood over Pookie holding a dead Cely in his arms. He pointed the still smoking gun at him and pulled the trigger.

Boom! Boom! Boom! Boom!

The repeated jumping in Toflon's hand sent Pookie into an eternal sleep with Cely still in his arms. Toflon made his exit out of the apartment building, which would prove to be a fatal mistake later.

Chapter 17

"I can't believe this kid is willing to come in and talk with us," Detective Tillman said, taking a sip of his like warm coffee.

"I'm not. You know how these young street punks are. They come in here to talk to us just to see what type of information we have on them, but that shit isn't happening today. Bryant Jones A.K.A BJ can never outthink two well-seasoned veterans like us," Detective Thomas said.

Frank Thomas and Andy Tillman have been on the Newport News Police force for over 17 years. They started out as partners 11 years ago on the narcotics squad, but with all the unsolved murders that took place in the city, they both thought they could serve the city of Newport News better if they joined the homicide branch. That was 5 years ago.

Detective Tillman was a hard nose cop. He hated drug dealers and the gunslingers. He really thought these kinds of people destroyed the city inside and out. Detective Thomas lost a mother to crack addiction and his younger brother Deon to gun violence. These two events motivated him to become a cop. It also fueled his hate towards drug dealers and those who used violence.

Detective Thomas was a big buff type of guy. He stood 6'3" and was physically in good shape at the age of 43, weighing 235 pounds. He had that leather looking type of facial skin. The kind that looked thick and was hard to cut.

On the other hand, Detective Tillman was somewhat the opposite of his partner. He was a God-fearing man. He was a married man with two kids, one boy and a precious girl. He was active in his community, coaching a basketball team for the Boys and Girl club. He also went and spoke at group homes and facilities for troubled youths.

Detective Tillman cared about the elevation of his black community. He felt if you weren't helping to build it, then you were helping tear it down. That's who he was out there, arresting and bringing people that broke the law and destroyed the community to justice.

"Excuse me, detectives. We have a Bryant Jones waiting in interview room three," the young rookie cop said as she stuck her head in their office.

"Okay. Thank you," Detective Thomas said, looking at the young rookie's backside as she walked away. Detective Tillman caught his partner staring and just shook his head.

"Come on, lover boy. We got us a suspect to go interview," Detective Tillman told him, standing up from his desk and slapping his partner on the back. Both detectives found BJ sitting in interview room three with his head on the table.

"Ms. Jones, I'm Detective Tillman and this is my partner, Detective Thomas." BJ lifted his head off the table and stared blankly at the detectives. The detective took a seat across the table from him in two folded chairs. Detective Thomas flopped a yellow legal note pad down on the table and removed a pen from his suit pocket.

"Thank you for coming down to the station," Detective Tillman said, making himself comfortable. BJ just nodded his head up and down. "So, you know why you are here, right?" he asked him.

"Yeah," BJ responded nonchalantly.

"Ok, well let me ask you a few questions so we can clear something up. Do you know a Robert Pulley?"

"Yeah, I know him but look, just give me that note pad and let me write out my confession," BJ said with a serious tone in his voice. The two detectives looked at each other in bewilderment. Detective Thomas hurried, pushing his note pad over to BJ.

BJ began to write. Detective Thomas nudged his partner on the leg, trying to get his attention that he needed to talk to him in the hallway. Both left BJ alone as they stepped out into the hallway. "Andy, I think this is the fastest confession we 've ever gotten," Detective Thomas said in excitement.

"Shit, Frank. I was thinking the same thing," Detective Tillman replied with a smile on his face. Detective Thomas looked through the small square window and found BJ staring straight ahead.

"Damn, that was quick," he said, entering back into the room with Detective Tillman on his heels.

"You finished already, Mr. Jones?" Detective Thomas inquired. BJ nodded his head up and down and pushed the note pad towards the detectives. Detective Thomas eagerly snatched it from the table. He read the small paragraph on the paper and became angry as fuck when he read BJ's confession. It read:

"I didn't kill Robert Pulley. I wasn't present at the hospital when Mr. Pulley was killed.
Bryant Jones

"What fucking type of games are you playing?" Detective Thomas spat, slamming the note pad down on the table before he stormed around the table and jacked BJ out of his chair by his collar.

"Bitch, get your fucking hands off me," BJ spoke directly in the detective's face. The interview door opened and a sexy figure occupied the doorway.

"Detective, get your hands off my client or I'll have you walking the beat until you retire." Detective Thomas immediately released BJ who smoothed his clothes out and sat down, crossing his legs like a boss.

The detective was quite familiar with the lawyer that stood in front of them. Misty Beck was the best defense attorney in Newport News and most sought out one too. Her performance in the courtroom was impeccable, almost high-level acting type. And to top it off, Misty Beck was a bombshell.

Her silky smoothed hair dropped down to the center of her backside. Her 38 C cups were perky and it seemed no matter the attire she wore, her nipples were always hard. She stood

5’7” with thick thighs and an apple bottom for an ass. Her Italian features were strong. She came in the room, threw her Louis Vuitton saddlebag on the table, and took a seat next to her client.

“Are you alright, Mr. Jones?” she asked. BJ nodded his head up and down with a smirk on his face, never breaking eye contact with Detective Thomas. “I see that you got my client’s confession,” she said, picking up the note pad off the table and examining it. Right then and there, the detectives knew they had been played. She tossed the confession back on the table in front of the detectives. “So, what do you have,” she asked, getting straight to the point.

“Uhum, uhum. Well, we wanted to talk to your client in reference of the Robert Pulley’s murder,” Detective Tillman said, shuddering. He wondered why BJ had hired this high-powered, high-priced lawyer just for them to talk to him.

“Okay, what about Robert Pulley?” she asked.

“Hold on, now. This is our interview. We asked the questions in here,” Detective Thomas blurted out angrily.

He didn’t care too much for the attorney. Ms. Beck had made him look like a fool more than once in the courtroom. The lawyer leaned over and whispered in BJ’s ear, giving him some legal advice on how to answer the question. BJ looked at the detectives.

“Like any brother, I was upset,” BJ replied. He and Ms. Beck had already gone over the do’s and don’ts before his interview.

“Well, was your anger enough to make you kill Mr. Pulley or was it the fact that Vanessa and Mr. Pulley were lovers and you didn’t approve of it?” asked Detective Tillman.

“Listen, I can’t take the dick for my sister, so I wasn’t mad about that.” Ms. Beck’s face turned beet red by his response. “But as far as being mad enough to kill him, then no. My anger wasn’t to that point,” BJ said, pulling the peach fuzz on his face.

"But it was enough for you to strike Mr. Pulley at the Riverside Hospital when you caught him coming out of Vanessa's room?" Detective Tillman drilled BJ with a smirk on his face. Ms. Beck leaned over again and spoke in BJ's ear, providing him with some more legal advice.

"My emotions got the best of me," he then simply replied.

"Ok, we see. Well, where were you the night of his murder?" Detective Tillman asked.

"You can check hospital surveillance to see if my client was there at the time of the murder." Ms. Beck interrupted.

"Why your client can't answer that?" Detective Tillman wanted to know.

"Because I'm informing him not to. What more do you want? He gave you a signed confession," she replied, standing to her feet and retrieving her Louis Vuitton saddlebag off the table. "Excuse me. Me and my client have somewhere to be," she advised. BJ stood up with his attorney. "And if you have any further questions, please contact me and I will contact my client." Ms. Beck held the door open for BJ to exit. He gave the detectives a broad smile and exited the room.

In the parking lot of the police station, BJ walked his attorney to her car. "Look, BJ. I advise you take a vacation and get away for a while. Let them bastards focus on someone else and stay out of trouble," she recommended.

"Ok, Ms. Beck. I hear you, but I'm going to give you another ten thousand on the retainer. I feel I'm going to need you down the line," he said.

"Alright, that would be fine, but you do know that Tashia already gave me ten thousand?"

"Yeah, I know but I just need to make sure that everything is in place in case something goes wrong in the near future," BJ stated sincerely.

"I can definitely understand that," she said, shaking BJ's hand and hopping in her navy-blue B.M.W 745 series. BJ walked to his money green Charger where Tashia was waiting. Ms. Beck's words ran through his head. *Take a vacation*. BJ got in the car and Tashia gave him a passionate kiss. She was happy to see her man walk out the police station.

"Yo, Tashia. We're getting ready to lay low for a minute. I'm getting ready to see who is who. Call them niggas Homicide and Bugg up and tell them that they locked me up. Tell them I said everything is going through until we find out what's going on. Baby, you got to call crying and everything. You have to be convincing," he said.

"Oh, if I don't know how to do nothing else, I know how to role play," she replied, picking up her phone and asking BJ for Homicide's number.

***

Both detectives were dumbfounded. "Frank, I feel like the kid knows something."

"Of course, he knows something. Why you think he hired the high-priced lawyer?" Thomas questioned.

"Yeah, that's puzzling to me, too. I wonder where he got the money to hire that attorney. I'm going to place a call to the narcotics branch and see what I can come up with," Detective Tillman said, placing BJ's confession in an evidence bag he was sending off to the lab for fingerprinting. He got up and walked out the interrogation room, following behind leather-faced Detective Thomas.

Chapter 18

"Yo, Toflon. What you doing tonight?" Fever asked, as he pulled in the Village projects better known as The VilI. The jet-black 500 Benz looked wet when the midday sun reflected off the sleek ride.

"I'm plan on getting with one of my dick eaters and smoke some purp and chill," Toflon said, checking the mirror on the passenger side.

"Well, we plan on falling through Magic City tonight to blow some money and fuck some bitches," Fever said, pulling to curb where a constant flow of weed was being sold.

"Man, I don't know about that, Fever. You know I like to keep my circle small," Toflon replied. "The crowd thing isn't for me."

"Come on, fam. Shit's going to be live," Fever said, trying to convince Toflon to hang out with the crew. Ever since he saved his life at the farmhouse, Fever had a different perspective of Toflon. He even started using Toflon to watch his back when he had to send Bear off to handle certain shit for him. Fever wanted to bring Toflon all the way in on the team. He even gave him an extra fifty thousand dollars for the work he put in at the farmhouse.

"I'll see, Fever," Toflon said. "Oh, there goes your boy." Toflon directed Fever's attention to a heavyset dude that was making his way to the Benz.

"What's happening, Fever," Doe Boy, said placing a Safeway bag full of money on Toflon lap through the passenger window.

"Nothing but that paper," Fever replied, while Toflon checked the bag of contents, seeing it contained nothing but green backs. Toflon was amazed at the type of money he witnessed Fever making. "I don't have to count this, do I?" Fever asked Doe Boy.

"Oh no, man. You know I'm always going to have all your bread at all times. It's not a dollar short," Doe Boy said.

Fever smiled at his statement. "Just how I like it. I prefer straight money over short money any day," Fever told him. "A'ight, hit me when you ready to see me again. Bear will be through here to holla at you," Fever said, pulling away from the curb. Fever and Toflon rode in silence listening to Drake successful. "You know that I put a ticket on the young nigga BJ's head," Fever stated, breaking the silence. Toflon looked at him in confusion.

"What you mean, fam? BJ is mines. I can handle that shit myself," Toflon said, eyeing Fever seriously. "What, you think that I'm not capable of handling that situation myself?"

Fever let out a deep breath. "Pfft! I know that you more than capable him. He's still going to be a dead muthafucka for what he did to my brother," he said, gritting his teeth in anger as he thought about how his brother was slain. He turned the Benz onto Jefferson Avenue. "I got plans to lock this whole fucking city down and I'm going to need you on my team to do it," Fever said.

"What that got to do with me killing BJ?" Toflon inquired, feeling like Fever was trying to play him.

"It means a lot. It means that we use our resources to handle BJ and move forward on getting this money. It means you need to come all the way on the team and get this money with me. How long you think that money from the farm job is going to last you? Huh? Well think about making that every two weeks. You'll be a millionaire in no time," Fever told him, trying to sell Toflon the idea on linking up with him.

He knew in due time the money was going to run low. He knew the money he could make with Fever he could use. "I tell you what, Fever. I'll get down with you, but I got to get hit BJ myself," Toflon stated firmly. "There was no way I'm going to let this bitch ass nigga get away with killing Butta and I want my gun to be the gun that pushes his shit back." Fever hid the smile on his face.

"I respect that and you can handle BJ. I'm going to call my shooter off tonight. But in the meantime, welcome to the team," Fever said, sticking a fist out he could Toflon a pound.

***

Vanessa was so excited to be home in her own bed and away from all the drama at the hospital. Tashia had her house cleaned up from top to bottom. Vanessa didn't have to lift a finger. Moocha was the one who usually took care of her every need. BJ had made sure of that. Plus, Vanessa wasn't going to just let anyone in her house to take care of her. She was familiar with Moocha and over the past few weeks, they had built an amazing bond. Tashia wasn't feeling Moocha's presence but it was about making Vanessa comfortable, so he held her peace.

"You need anything, sis?" BJ asked her as he walked into his sister's room, interrupting her from watching *The Steve Harvey Morning* show.

"Ummm, yeah. Come in and shut the door," she said, sitting up in her queen-sized bed. She wrung her hands together. She was nervous as to how this conversation was going to turn out with her brother.

"What's good, Nessa?" BJ said, kissing his sister on the cheek and taking a seat on the edge of her bed.

"I want to talk to you about something really serious and no matter how much you think it may hurt me, please tell me the truth," she said, watching BJ's body language.

"Okay, sis. Holla at ya bruh."

Vanessa reached out and grabbed one of BJ's hand. "The chain I took from the safe, did it belong to a dude named Block?" Vanessa inquired, searching his eyes for the truth.

BJ closed his eyes for a minute. He had to quickly weigh his options. Apparently, Vanessa knew more about the chain than he wanted her to know. This was his sister and he almost lost her once, so he wasn't going to lose her over a lie. "Yeah, the chain used to belong to Block, but originally it belongs to

Lil Chris's brother, Peanut. Block and his people killed Peanut and took the chain." BJ said with a hint of sadness in his voice.

"So, how did you get the chain?" Vanessa questioned.

BJ let out sigh, rubbing his hand over his waves and face. "Pssssss, Lil Chris found out that Block killed his brother. So, Lil Chris killed Block once he found out that him, Skalez, 40 had something to do with killing his brother. He was on a mission to kill Skalez and 40, but 40 ended up getting locked up before he could kill him. While he was locked up, we caught Skalez slipping, so we robbed and killed him. The night we robbed Skalez, somehow, he'd gotten the drop on us and came out of nowhere with a gun, killing Lil Chris. But it was me that killed Skalez," BJ confessed, not knowing what type of reaction he was going to get out of her.

Vanessa just stared at him as if she was seeing him through a different set of eyes. BJ felt like he needed to keep talking, the silence in the room was awkward. "I took the chain from Lil Chris. Lil Chris was my best friend. The chain was all I had left of him." BJ eyes welled up, thinking about his childhood friend laid out with bullet holes in his chest.

"So, why did you kill 40? He didn't know you killed Skalez or Block." He could see tears creeping up in her eyes.

"He did know, Nessa. He was going to kill me. He figured out that I killed Skalez."

"But I loved him, BJ!" Vanessa yelled, squeezing his hand.

"It was going to be me or him Vanessa and that nigga wasn't shit. When we pulled that caper on Lance, he shitted on me. He took the lion's share and gave me a punk ass five thousand dollars."

"I don't give a fuck about no Lance robbery. 40 was my life!" Vanessa started to cry. "I finally found a man that truly loves me and you killed him!" she screamed out.

"Shhhhh, keep your voice down. Tashia and Moocha are in the other room. I didn't kill 40 at the hospital, but I don't give a damn if he's dead." BJ's statement sent Vanessa over the top.

"Get the fuck out! Get out my house! I hate you! I hate you heartless ass! Get the fuck out!" Vanessa screamed at the top of her lungs. Tashia and Moocha heard the commotion and entered the room. BJ and Vanessa locked eyes like two raging dogs. He stood up with fire in his eyes. He was furious she was choosing 40 over him. He walked to the door where Tashia and Moocha were standing. He turned on his heels and said, "Remember this, Nessa. At the end of the day and no matter what, we are family," BJ said.

"Boy, fuck you and that family shit!" Vanessa said at BJ's back with hate in her words.

Chapter 19

BJ came out of Vanessa's house with Tashia following closely behind him. They jumped in his money green Charger and backed out the driveway. He hit the gas pedal a little too hard, causing the high-powered car to spin a little that left a burnt rubber in the street.

The driver of the Dodge Magnum wondered what had gotten BJ all hot and bothered. He could tell by the way he stormed out of the house and burned off down the street, that something was going on with BJ. He started up his car, following behind him. He'd been tailing BJ off and on for the last few days trying to decide when was the best time and best possible way to kill him.

***

"Come on, girl. It's going to be alright," Moocha said, holding a crying Vanessa. Moocha caressed her back as she cried her eyes out. The feeling that she felt being in Moocha's arms was comfortable. She felt like she was her only friend in the world.

"I can't believe that BJ killed Rob!" Vanessa said through tears. Even though BJ didn't admit to killing him, Vanessa could tell her brother had something to do with it by the look he had in his eyes. Moocha continued to rock Vanessa back and forth. She didn't really want to comment on the statement Vanessa had just made. "Now I have no one to love me."

"What? Vanessa, cut that nonsense out. Sure, you have someone that loves you. I love you." Vanessa pulled away from her, tilting her head to the side. She looked into Moocha's eyes and smiled.

"Awwwww, you are so sweet," Vanessa said, wiping tears from her eyes.

"No, Vanessa. You are the one that's sweet and beautiful. You know that love don't always have to come from the affection of a man," Moocha said as she traced Vanessa's face with her hands, taking her index finger and outlining her lips. Out of instinct, Vanessa took her finger in her mouth. She sucked on it and closed her eyes, savoring its taste.

Moocha removed her finger and replaced it with her tongue. Vanessa resisted slightly, then she hungrily took Moocha' s tongue into her mouth. Their kiss seemed like it lasted for an eternity. Vanessa had never indulged in any girl on girl acts, but for some reason at this moment and with this particular person, the act felt good. Vanessa could feel the heat from her womanhood rising a few degrees.

"Mmmmm, mami. You taste so good," Moocha said with a handful of Vanessa's breasts. She caressed her nipples through the fabric of her shirt. Vanessa stuck her tongue deeper into Moocha's mouth, enjoying the texture of her tongue. "Can I make you feel good, Vanessa?" Moocha asked.

"Mhmmm. Yea, please!" Vanessa cried out in between kisses. Moocha pulled away from her and undid her jeans, letting them fall to the floor. She then pulled her shirt over her head and in the matter of seconds, standing before Vanessa naked.

Vanessa was overwhelmed with how turned on she was seeing Moocha's naked body. She bit down on her bottom lip at the sight of Moocha's swollen melons. She helped Vanessa out of her clothes. She shied away, covering the healing scars on her chest with her hands. Moocha removed her hands and eased her back on the bed.

"No, mami. Don't hide anything. I want to see all of you. I think that you are beautiful, scars and all. I'm going to make you feel good. Are you ready, mami?" Moocha questioned her seductively, taking a second to stare into Vanessa's brown eyes. "Just relax, mami." Vanessa didn't reply. She just stared lustfully into her eyes.

While Moocha placed one soft and wet kiss after another on her lips and neck, Moocha made it her responsibility to stimulate Vanessa's supple nipples and ripe breasts. Vanessa's breathing instantly became strained by the way Moocha licked and traced her nipples with her fingers. The way her body was responding to Moocha's touch told her that she was highly experienced in pleasing a woman.

It took no time for Moocha to reach in between Vanessa's dripping wet thighs. Once her lips and tongue began to work its magic, Vanessa opened her legs up wider, giving her full access to her goodies. She looked down at her face buried deeply in her pussy. Vanessa was highly aroused at the mere sight of Moocha feasting on her love box.

"Oh Moocha, baby!" Vanessa said short of breath. "I want to taste you, too," Vanessa said. Moocha lifted her head and flashed a smile smeared with Vanessa's love juices.

"You want me to get in the sixty-nine position, mami?"

Vanessa couldn't respond. All she could do was hold tightly to the back of Moocha's mane while she stabbed her tongue in and out her pussy, making number eight figures around her clit and love hole. Vanessa's legs clamped down on her head.

Moocha was definitely in her element, but she was anxious to be the first woman Vanessa tasted. This desire alone forced her to easily twist her voluptuous body around. She mounted Vanessa's face while she still devoured her pussy.

Moocha's fat chocolate muffin hung directly over Vanessa's face, emitting a powerful and erotic aroma. Vanessa was hesitant at first. She didn't know how to tell Moocha she wanted to taste her. She guessed she was caught up in the moment, but Vanessa did it anyway.

She slowly parted Moocha's ass cheeks, getting a grade "A" view of her honey-glazed honey pot. Vanessa told herself, *I'm going to do it how I would want it done to me.* She then placed her lips on Moocha's pot of honey and the feeling instantly felt divine.

"Oh my God, you taste so good. Your pussy feels like it belongs in my mouth," Vanessa said. "I never would have thought—" Vanessa stopped herself, slipping her tongue into Moocha's love nest.

Moocha was forced to smile. This wasn't the first female she had turned out and she definitely knew Vanessa wasn't going to be her last. She kept her arms wrapped around her toned legs, continuing to suck on her pussy like it was going out of style. They both feasted upon each other like two savage hogs. Nothing in the world mattered at the time.

"Oh, Moocha! I—I'm cuuuummming," Vanessa called out, her whole body beginning to tremble under Moocha.

Moocha felt her own orgasm coming, grinding harder into Vanessa's soft tongue. Both women came as if something inside of them commanded them to cum at the same time. Moocha got up and laid next to Vanessa with her body still trembling body. Vanessa was breathless. Moocha gave her a few pecks on the lips and got up to go get some water.

She watched Moocha's backside, smiling at what she saw. Moocha had ass for days. The beautiful artwork she had on her back enhanced her beauty. The tattoo was a red rose, growing out the crack of concrete that wrapped around the thorny rose stem with a banner that said, "In the Memory of L".

Five minutes later, Moocha returned with a cold glass of water that Vanessa drank in its entirety. Mooch jumped back into bed with her. "You okay, girl?" she asked, looking into Vanessa's eyes for any sign of regret. She saw nothing. That meant to her, it was meant to be.

"I'm okay. Just shocked I did all that my first time," Vanessa admitted, giggled. She really didn't know how to title her experience.

"Sometimes things happen that feel right or good. We have a tendency to put our all into it. This is one of those situations," Moocha replied.

"Yeah, I guess so," Vanessa said, letting out a sigh as a sad expression appeared on her face. Moocha noticed the change in her facial expression.

"Hey, hey. What's the sad face for all of the sudden?" Moocha questioned.

"I just don't understand my brother at times. One day, he's this dirty little kid, but the next day, he's this drug dealer and he's killing people," Vanessa said. "I understand. This is a dog eats dog world out there. I just hope he knows that when you live by the gun, the streets will clap back. I hate he did that to Rob."

"I understand your concerns, Vanessa." Moocha paused. "I had a husband that was in the streets." Moocha eyes watered. "One night, I came home and I found him and our 6-year-old dead. The robbers couldn't find the drugs because they weren't in the house. They killed my family. I moved here from New York with my brother L and four years later, here I was dealt the same fate." Moocha wiped her eyes.

Vanessa felt bad for Moocha. She held her in her arms trying to bring her some comfort. She felt that since Moocha had shared something personal with her, she was obligated to share something personal with her, too.

"You know that BJ had Rob killed because he shorted him some money from a caper they pulled together. BJ told me after they robbed some guy named Lance, that Rob gave BJ a small portion of the money, but he kept the lion's share of the money from the caper," Vanessa said as Moocha's body stiffened. Vanessa felt the tension. "Are you okay, Moocha?"

"Yeah, mami. I just hate to hear about peopled being killed. Plus, dudes in the street be acting stupid when they find out someone knows their business, especially when its murder. So, please don't say nothing to BJ about you telling me about him and 40's situation."

"Oh, you don't have to worry about that, Moocha. I promise you that, "Vanessa said.

"Well, Vanessa. I have to get ready for work," she told her, getting out of the bed. She then stepped into her jeans and pulled her shirt back over her head.

"Are you coming back after your shift is over? I don't want to spend the night but myself," Vanessa said with lust in her voice.

"Of course, I would," Moocha stated with a fake smile. She then kissed Vanessa on the lips before she walked out the room.

Chapter 20

Wallo poured himself another shot of Hennessey. He had been drinking heavy over the past few days. He did this often when he thought about his cousin Skalez and now his short-term partner was gone, another devastating blow for him. But what enraged him was Tashia teaming up with BJ, going against Skalez, Block and 40.

"Scandalous ass bitch!" Wallo spoke to himself. He downed another shot of Hennessey, refilling the shot glass with another one. *It all made sense*, Wallo thought.

Tashia was part of the caper they pulled on Lance. That was obvious because she came and got the counting machine from him the night they had pulled the caper. She knew Block, 40 and Skalez had money. She also knew that BJ was down with the lick.

He figured she must have gotten into the young nigga their heads, influencing them to hit Block, Skalez and 40. Wallo downed the shot of Hennessey, throwing the glass against the wall that shattered into pieces. "This fucking bitch been shady all this fucking time," he said, raising his voice.

"My cousin played fair with you bitch and you set him up and had him killed. Then you turn around and fuck the young nigga that killed him?" Wallo spoke to no one but himself. The drink had him playing out the scenario of what happened to his cousin and friends. "It will be a cold day in hell before I let you and that faggot ass nigga get away with killing my cousin," Wallo said, picking his 9-millmimter Ruger up off the couch that was next to him.

***

"I can't believe this nigga got me sitting on hot ass Jefferson Avenue with three ounces on me. Where the fuck this nigga at?" Moe-B asked himself, while nervously scanning his surroundings. Moe-B hated to sit in one spot with all that coke on him. He saw Hammer's blue Tahoe pull up not too far behind the cabstand. He tapped his horn twice to get his attention. Hammer hopped out his truck, making his way over to Moe-B's Charger and got in.

"What's up Moe?"

"Nigga, it's you. That's what's up. You got a nigga sitting on hot ass Jefferson with three ounces and you have the nerve to be late?" Moe-B said with his face balled up.

"Man, just chill the fuck out and be cool," Hammer replied, pulling a wad of cash out his pocket. The men froze as a police car cruised past them.

The cops in the car looked in their direction. Moe-B watched him out of the corner of his eye. The cop kept creeping past them without stopping. Moe-B watched him cruise down the avenue through side view mirror.

Once he felt comfortable, he resumed back to business. "Here, nigga," he said, passing Hammer a brown bag. He quickly examined the contents in the bag.

"Oh, yeah. That's what I'm talking about," Hammer said, passing Moe-B the wad of money he held in his hand. He could tell the money was short.

"Hold up, Hammer. Let me count this scrilla."

"Man, you ain't got to count it. That's two grand. I'm going to hit you with the rest when I re-up tomorrow."

"Nigga, do I look like a sucka? You had me bring three ounces and you only got money for two?" Moe-B reached in his waistline and quickly removed his .357 Python. He backhanded him in the mouth, causing his head to snap back with force.

Hammer grabbed his mouth. He could feel the jagged edges of his broken teeth on his tongue. "You bitch ass nigga, trying me like I'm some sucka!" he yelled, bringing the gun down again on top of Hammer's head. He gave him a three-inch gash on the left side of his forehead, the blow making him disoriented.

Moe-B pressed the large cannon to the side of Hammer's face, penning it between the passenger's door and the barrel of his gun. Moe-B patted him down and removed a chrome Smith and Western 45 with an extended clip. He smiled at his new weapon. He continued to search Hammer, going through his pockets.

He removed larger wad of cash from Hammer's pocket, becoming furious. "Bitch as nigga, you playing games, fam?" Moe-B clunked Hammer in the head again with the gun. Moe-B leaned across Hammer and opened the door on the passenger's side. His weight was against the door, forcing it open. He fell out onto the busy sidewalk of Jefferson Avenue. Moe-B closed the door and put the Charger in drive, pulling out into traffic.

"I can't believe Hammer's sucka ass tried to pull this stunt with me!" Moe-B spoke out loud. "I don't know why these niggas can't be straight business. They always putting some bullshit in the game," he mumbled. Grabbing the brown bag that was in between the console of the car, he put the gun he took from Hammer and dropped it in the bag with the work before he threw it on the passenger's seat.

Moe-B checked his rearview mirror only to see the police car that drove by him and Hammer was now behind him. His heart started to race. He took a deep breath, trying not to panic as he drove down Jefferson. Moe-B fished his phone out his pocket and hit a number on speed dial.

"Hello." A female voice could be heard on speakerphone.

"Kay-Kay!" Moe-B's voice blurted through the phone.

"Oh hey, baby," she said in a better tone, recognizing her boo's voice.

"You in the house, right?" Moe-B asked, glancing into his mirror. He was checking to see if the police car was still behind him.

"Yes, Moe-B. I'm in the house. You coming through?" The red and blue lights on top of the police car lit up.

"Look, I need you to come outside now. I"m headed towards the G now. I got the police following me. Hit the cut by your building and walk down the street. I'm in the Charger. I'm going to throw a brow bag out the window. You get the bag and haul ass in the house. It's some money in the bag, too. It's yours. Just call my Uncle Homicide Jack and let him know the deal," Moe-B said, placing the money he got off Hammer in the bag along with the .357 and the 45. Kay-Kay threw on a hoodie and made her way out the door.

"Okay, baby. I'm already walking through the cut heading towards the back street. I'm standing in between the buildings," she said. She was that ride and die chick every man wanted, but none gave her the time of day because she wasn't that dime everyone wanted. Kay-Kay was a fat girl. Moe-B saw her worth, often coming through to show her some love and dick her down.

Moe-B pushed down hard on the gas pedal, bringing the Hemi engine to life as it pushed the white Charger down Jefferson Avenue towards Stuart Gardens better known as The G.

The G was coming up on Moe-B's right. The police car was in high pursuit, tailing Moe-B with his sirens blowing. Moe-B faked a left, making a hard right instead. That maneuver brought some distance between him and the police car.

He drove passed The G doing 85. He turned on the back street behind the projects and right on time like the true gangsta girl she was, Kay-Kay was standing by the cut with her hoodie pulled tightly over her head. Moe-B power rolled the passenger's window down and without stopping, he tossed the brown bag out the window.

Kay-Kay acted like a wide receiver. She caught the bag in midair and took off running. The cop didn't know what to do. He wasn't sure if he should stop and chase the person in the hoodie who caught the bag or continue to chase the Charger. He chose to chase Moe-B.

Moe-B wanted to put some distance between him and Kay-Kay, but he knew needed to pull over where they were because the Newport News police would beat your ass for running them.

He made his way back around to the front of the projects. By this time, there was three more police cars behind the one that was already chasing him. He pulled up in the middle of Stuart Gardens Projects, bringing the car to a halt. The police cars surrounded him. Moe-B looked out through the windshield. He tapped the gas pedal and rear the engine. The whole projects came out to see what all the commotion was about.

"You, in the white car, roll down the window, turn the car off and drop the keys out the window," an officer demanded through the loud speaker of his car. Moe-B came into compliance and obeyed the officer's instructions. "Now, open the car door from the outside and get out with your hands in the air and face away from us." Moe-B followed the officer's second set of demands. "Now, lay down on the ground." Moe-B laid on the pavement. The officers rushed him at gunpoint. One officer cuffed him.

"What was in the bag you threw out the window," the officer asked.

"I don't know nothing about a bag, sir," Moe-B replied and smiled as he stared at Kay-Kay, standing in the crowd of the spectators talking on her phone. He winked at her and she blew him a kiss.

Chapter 21

LJ pulled up into Riley Circle off 16th and Jefferson Avenue. He made his way out his black Buick and headed over to where Fever and a few of his peoples were indulged in a craps game. "Bet nine or five niggas," a tall skinny dude with a long beard said as he shook a red pair of dice.

"Bet! Bet a C-note, nigga. You don't nine or five," a short muscular dude with dreads said, dropping a one hundred bill on the ground. The skinny dude matched his fader's money by dropping a crispy one-hundred-dollar bill on top of the one hundred dollar that was on the ground.

"I like the nine or five," Fever called. "I like it for a thousand."

"I don't like the nine or five," LJ said, walking up on the crap game." Fever looked at Bear sideways for letting a nigga like LJ get up on him and the crap game without putting him on point. Bear was slipping. Toflon would have never let that happen. Fever dropped a G stack on the ground and LJ followed suit.

The skinny dude held the dice high in the air and shook the dice. They clicked in his hand. The small crowd that attended the game was quiet as the skinny dude released the dice from his hand on the sidewalk. The dice bounce and danced. One of the dice stopped on a six, but the other one kept spinning in a circle.

It seemed like the dice spun forever. The dice shooter held his breath. Then it finally stopped and landed on one. "Fuck!" the skinny dude yelled out. He couldn't believe he crapped out. LJ and the guy with the Muslim beard picked up their winnings.

"LJ, you are one luck muthafucka," Fever said. "Come take a walk with me," Fever said as they headed up the block while Bear became their shadow, giving them enough space to speak in private. "Tell me something good, LJ," he said, putting a backwood in his mouth before he lit it.

"Well, there ain't much to tell. The nigga BJ hasn't surfaced and his muscle hasn't introduced me to him yet," LJ answered in a mumbled whisper while his head stayed on a swirl.

"Damn, I was hoping you would have taken care of BJ by now. I need this shit to be off my plate so I can put my other plans into play," Fever said, hitting the purp deeply then passing it to LJ.

"Shit, who you telling. I want this done. I'm trying to collect that hundred thousand you got on his head," LJ stated as thick clouds of smoke seeped out his nose.

"Listen!" Fever said, stopping in his tracks and facing LJ. "There's never been a nigga in this city that you couldn't locate. What makes this nigga BJ different?" he asked.

"There's nothing different. I been waiting on Homicide Jack to plug me in with him." LJ took another hit of the purp.

"Old head, I need you to go all in on this thing. Ain't no young nigga or nobody in this city going to clap my brother and walk around to tell about it. So, handle that fucking nigga or I'll tell ever hitter in the city that I got a brick on that nigga's head and let the chips fall when they may."

"Fever, no need to do all that. Them niggas are going to be reckless and that shit is going to bring heat," LJ said, letting another thick cloud of smoke out his nose.

"Well handle it and stop fucking around!" Fever told him, snatching the backwood from him as spent on his heels and walked back towards the dice game.

Two black GMCs pulled fast into Riley Circle. Seconds later, masked men jumped out with assault rifles and small machine looking guns.

Pop! Pop! Pop! Pop! Boch! Boch! Boch! Boch!

The gunshots interrupted the dice game. Fever drew his 45 from the small of his back and ducked behind an old model Toyota. He could hear the bullets hitting the car. His men scattered like roaches. The tall skinny dude only took two steps towards safety before a bullet ripped through the back of his scalp, sending him to an early death. The short guy with the long Muslim beard was about to get his gun out and return fire.

Blucka! Blucka! Blucka! Blucka!

The 9-millimeter Ruger gave him enough coverage to reach the side of the project's building. The projects took on gunfire from the eight gunmen. They were advancing towards Fever. LJ watched from the doorway of another building. He could see Bear hiding behind an Astro van, but Bear couldn't see him.

He saw Bear reach in his pocket and pullout his phone. He made a quick call and placed it back in his pocket. LJ was a vet. He knew something wasn't right with this picture. He normally didn't get into other niggas' beef unless he was paid to do so, but he couldn't just let these muthafuckas gun Fever down like this while his man Bear bitched up.

LJ pulled the Glock 40 off his hip and took a deep breath. He then stepped out from the doorway of the apartment building where he was. He let off three quick shots.

Boom! Boom! Boom!

One hit one of the masked men in the throat, dropping him. He clutched his neck trying to stop the blood from gushing out. The other two shots stopped another gunmen in his tracks. Bullets from his Glock 40 found home in the center mass of the gunmen's chest. Bear could see LJ now. He pulled his 44 Magnum and pointed at the one of the gunman, pulling its trigger.

Boooom! Boooom! Booom! The large cannon roared.

Bear didn't hit anything. Fever took this opportunity to run to another car behind him. He popped his head up just as one of the gunmen was turning his way.

Boom! Boom! Boom!

Fever's 45 opened up, knocking a chuck of flesh out the gunmen's shoulder and thigh. The masked man drop his gun and it skipped across the pavement. Finally, the projects regrouped and help was coming. At the top of the building where LJ was, a young dude opened fire from a crack head's window.

LJ made his way over to Fever. The other gunmen started retreating to their trucks. You could hear sirens in the distance as the black GMC trucks got away. LJ knew he needed to get out of there. "You alright, Fever?" LJ asked him, still clutching his smoking Glock 40.

"Yeah, good looking out but get the fuck outta here," Fever told him as he ran over to the gunman that laid on the concrete, holding his shoulder and thigh. Fever bent down and removed the mask from the gunman's face. It was Paulie. "So, Aymir sent you, huh?" Fever said, smiling.

"I should have killed you when I had a chance out at the farm house," Paulie replied with disgust in his voice. The sirens were getting closer.

"I know. I was thinking the same thing myself," Fever said, lifting the 45 and dropping a slug in his head. Fever and Bear got to the Benz, making it out of Riley Circle just before Newport News' finest came sliding into the projects.

Chapter 22

Two days later, Homicide Jack sat on the corner of 16th and Jefferson Avenue. He puffed on a Newport 100, waiting for Kay-Kay's chubby ass to bring him whatever Moe-B had left for him to pick up. He flicked the cigarette out the window, blowing smoke out his nose as he listened to Drake.

Homicide snapped his fingers and bobbed his head to the beat of the music. "Damn, this nigga Drake is talking that shit!" Homicide Jack spoke to himself. He finally saw Kay-Kay walking up. She didn't look half ass bad for a chubby bitch.

She had big breasts and curvy thighs. Kay-Kay was 7 years older than Moe-B. She stood 5'5" with big round breasts that bounced and shook like they were full of Jello. He always saw her at night, but now he was seeing her in the daytime. He saw she was very pretty. She just needed to lose the gut. Kay-Kay moved awkwardly with the brown bag in her hand.

What the fuck this bitch got, Homicide Jack thought to himself. He tapped the horn to get Kay-Kay's attention. She made her way to the car and got in on the passenger's side.

"What's up, pretty woman?" Homicide Jack said, putting some charm in his voice.

"I'm good. Just missing my boo," Kay-Kay said, passing Homicide Jack the brown bag.

"I need to holla at you," Homicide said.

"Okay, what is it?" Kay-Kay questioned.

"I need you to pass by Moe-B's mother house, pick her up and take her to the jail to get him." Kay-Kay smiled at the thought of seeing Moe-B. She knew he was younger but the way he acted and made her feel mentally and physically, proved his age was not a factor.

"Okay, I'll go get her and we can go get Moe-B together."

"A'ight, cool. Beautiful, here's some money for your trouble." Homicide pulled some bills out his pocket and passed them to her. She took the money and stuffed it in between her breasts. Kay-Kay caught Homicide Jack staring. The two locked eyes giving each other a look that said, "try me" but neither were willing to make the first move.

Homicide Jack shifted in his seat as his third leg began to wake up. It had been awhile since he had some young tender pussy. He shifted in his seat once more, causing the bag on his lap make a metal clinking sound. Homicide curiously opened up the bag. He saw two guns and three ounces of hard white in the bag, breaking him out in sweat.

"What the fuck? I'm sitting on hot ass Jefferson Avenue with this shit on my lap," he said out loud. He started looking around to see if anybody was watching them. His sudden paranoia made her start looking around for unwanted eyes. Homicide Jack knew then he had to get to moving.

"Ummm, look. Go holla at Moe-B moms and go grab that nigga. When he gets out, tell to get with me ASAP."

"Okay, I will," she said, getting out the car and making her way back down Jefferson Avenue. Homicide Jack then pulled out into traffic.

***

Fever sat his on his back porch in his rocking chair of his Norfolk home. He slowly rocked back and forth thinking about the shootout in Riley Circle. He twirled a 45 round in between his fingers on his right hand as he sipped from the fifth of Hennessey. Fever had been in the game a minute and he didn't get by and make it this far by being blind to shit.

He knew someone had to inform Aymir's men of his whereabouts. He just didn't know who. *Was it Bear, LJ, Duck or someone that lived on in Riley Circle,* he asked himself. Fever took another sip of the Hennessey and twirled the 45 bullet between his fingers once more. This revelation would slow his takeover of the city's weed trade, but he had to first smoke out whoever was amongst his ranks committing treason.

Chapter 23

"The lawyer is doing everything she can to get BJ out of jail. She told me they don't have anything on him. They're just holding him to shake him up a bit," Tashia said, speaking into the phone.

"Okay. When is he going back to court?" Bugg asked.

"Ummm, Ms. Beck told me in the next two days."

"Well, keep me posted on everything," Bugg replied.

"I will, but when I talked to him this morning, he wanted to know did you holla at the family about putting the food on the table?" Tashia asked, talking in codes. She really was asking if he talked to the connect about the product.

"Oh, yeah. Everything is everything on the family. Everyone is happy and full," Bugg stated, letting her know everything was good.

"Ok, I will let him know," she said, disconnecting the call. She smiled at BJ as he laid in the large hotel bed at the "W" in Washington D. He was butt naked, slowly stroking his dick. She stood at the foot of the bed in her own birthday suit looking thicker than a tree stump. "BJ, look at you? You so damn nasty," she told him, crawling in bed with him and taking control of his manhood with her own hands.

"This is the way you like me, right?" BJ replied with a devilish grin on his face. He kissed her deeply. Tashia's slippery tongue and soft tender hand job she was giving him enhanced his erection. Precum oozed out the head of his manhood, bringing lubrication to his love muscle. She straddled him, easing down on him easily.

BJ was well endowed for his young age. Tashia worked herself completely down on him with perfection. Her big round ass cheeks rested on BJ's thighs. He gave her right butt cheek a solid smack.

Wack!

"Argggggggh!" Tashia cried out as she begun to slowly rotate her hips in a circular motion. BJ bit down on his bottom lip as they intensely stared at each other. Tashia worked her hips a little faster, coming up off the dick a little further. This caused her ass cheeks to make a popping sound as they hit his thighs.

Pat! Pat! Pat!

"Oh, BJ. I can feel it in my stomach," she moaned out in pleasure. BJ grabbed her hips and arched his back off the bed, pushing his manhood deeper inside of her.

"Agggrrh! Mmmm, baby!" Tashia really began bouncing hard on his love stick. "I'm about to cum, baby!" she cried out, rocking back and forth on his dick. BJ pumped harder, matching her every stroke.

"Cum, baby. Cum for me. Bring it to daddy," BJ coached her, pumping harder into her love cave. Tashia's breasts bounced and banged into his face with every thrust he gave her.

"Owwwww, baaaaaaaabby! I'm cuuumming!" Tashia yelled out. BJ could feel her extra syrupy release trickling down his shaft and on to his balls. He felt his own orgasm coming.

"I'm about to cum, Tashia. Here it comes," BJ spoke in between breaths. She could feel his dick expanding.

She hopped off his dick, coming off him with a nasty sucking sound. She rushed and placed his glistening dick in her mouth, slowly swallowing his gooey cum. "Grrrrrr!" BJ growled loudly, releasing his load into her mouth.

Tashia milked him dry. She came up smiling as she wiped her mouth like she had just ate her favorite dish. She laid beside him, letting her fingertips dance in his sweat that covered his chest. BJ was breathing hard as he tried to catch his breath. "I love you, BJ," she told him.

"I love you, too, baby."

***

Detective Tillman and Detective Thomas sat in their office looking dumbfounded. They didn't have a lead or a suspect in the Robert Pulley murder. They couldn't believe that the camera on the fifth floor of the Riverside Hospital was out of service for 45 days, leaving them without any footage of the murderer.

"Thomas, every bone in my body tells me that this guy Bryant Jones was involved," Detective Tillman said from his desk, breaking his partner out of his trance.

"I'm with you on that Tillman, but we need something to prove that he had something to do with the murder, "Detective Thomas said, propping his size 12s on top of his desk as he locked his fingers behind his head.

"I think we should bring him in for another interview one more time and apply some pressure to his ass," Detective Tillman suggested, balling up his large hand into a fist and squeezing it tightly in frustration.

"Yeah, that's smart but the kid would have his high-priced lawyer all over our ass, too, e specially if we pull him in without her permission. We should just follow his ass for a few days and see what we can come up with," Detective Thomas replied, letting out a deep breath.

"That might—" *Ring-ring.* They were interrupted, hearing the phone ring on Detective Tillman's desk. He picked up and said, "Detective Tillman here."

"Hey, Tillman. This is Lieutenant Masion from narcotics. I got some info about your boy Bryant Jones AKA BJ."

"Okay!" he said, sitting up in his chair.

"Well, the little fucker has been under the radar, but the word from my C.I. is that BJ is an up and coming star in the hood."

"Yeah, is that what your confidential informant said?" Detective Tillman became excited.

"Yep, and that's not all. The C.I. also informed me that a month ago, there was a real bad shootout in front of this so-called trap house on twenty-fourth that left two dead. A David 'Butta' Buckers and Marcel Tate known as Lil Tate."

"Any connection to BJ and the deceased?" asked Detective Tillman. Detective Thomas listened intensively to his partner's conversation.

"No, there's no connection, but the informant said he thinks one of the deceased worked for BJ. He just can't confirm if this true or not." Hearing this, Detective Tillman gritted his teeth. He knew he had just hit another dead end with BJ.

"Okay. Thanks for the intel, Lieutenant Masion. I owe you one."

"You're welcome. You know one hand washes the other in our line of business," he stated, hanging the phone up. Detective Tillman placed the desk phone back on its cradle and looked at his partner. "That was Lieutenant Masion out of the narcotics unit. He just gave me a run down on Bryant Jones. It appears that we don't have shit on him. Masion talked to a C.I. who said he's an up and coming star in the drug game. Still, we can't do shit about that because we work homicide, not narcotics. What we do know is that he paid for Ms. Beck with drug money," Detective Tillman said.

Detective Thomas just shook his head and mumbled, "Unfucking believable."

***

BJ and Tashia walked hand in hand, as they strolled through the DC National Aquarium. Tashia loved being with him. It had been a while since they'd spent some one-on-one time with one another. BJ getting shot shook her to the core. She really couldn't deal with the fact that 40 tried to kill him. "Oh my God, BJ. Look at that beautiful ass Angel fish," she said in awe.

"I see it, baby. It's beautiful just like you are," he replied, smiling as he tried to win some cool points with his love. He fore played his words so when he got her back to the "W" hotel, she would already be soaking wet and ready to go.

"Awww, boo. You always know the right thing to say," she cooed, placing a peck on BJ's lips before leading him down towards the small shark tank. "Baby, did you get a chance to talk to Vanessa?" she asked, locking hands with him and pulling him closer.

"Naw, I really don't know what to say to her, Tashia. I never thought she would go against me," BJ admitted, releasing her hand. He wrapped his arm around her waist as they stopped in front of the shark tank.

"I don't think she's going against you, BJ. She's just hurt and disappointed."

"Disappointed? What, disappointed that 40 didn't kill me? It seemed like she was concerned about 40 being her lover more than him wanting me dead," BJ said, shaking his head from left to right.

"Baby, look at me!" she said, facing BJ as she wrapped her arms around his waist. "Vanessa is your sister. She's just hurt right now. She'll never go against you. It may seem like that now, but she is very emotional right now. She was shot twice, lost her baby in the process and the man she loved was murdered despite the fact that you and him were gunning for one another. She still had feelings for 40 and feelings like that just don't disappear overnight."

BJ looked in Tashia's eyes and heard her words of sincerity. "Yeah, I hear ya but Nessa acting like I'm not ever her brother," BJ protested, really not wanting to give in to Tashia's argument.

"Ok, but you're still her brother. Vanessa will get over this but you still have to do your brotherly duties and check up on her," she replied, kissing him on the chin.

BJ let out a sigh. "Ok, I will but I'm going to give her a few more days to herself."

"Good, that's reasonable. Plus, I'm not getting married without your sister being at our wedding."

"What? You're tripping, Tashia! What if she says no?" BJ asked.

"Well, then you need to make sure she says yes," she said, easing her hand between her and BJ, grabbing a handful of his dick. He just shook his head in amazement at her. Women will always go straight to the dick to make their man do something he doesn't want to do or is impossible for him to do. And in this case, this was one of those situations.

Chapter 24

Toflon casually walked through MacArthur Mall. He'd been spending money on some footwear. He had just stepped out of Footlocker with two pair of Jordans, a black and white pair of Air Max and a pair of black Timberland boots. He had plans to hit up a few other stores, but his stomach got to growling. So, he stopped by the Hot Pretzel stand that sat directly in front of Amyir Jeweler's store.

Toflon ordered two large pretzels with honey mustard on them. A pair of cuties that walked past the pretzel stand caught his attention. The tall, bowlegged redbone caught him staring at her. In response, she smiled seductively at him. Her friend saw the two-eye fucking each other. "You might as well say something to each other before your eye balls dry up from staring at one another without blinking."

The redbone scolded her friend. "Girl, mind your business and stay out of mines." Toflon laughed at the duo. "Hello, my name is Rose and this silly girl right here is Penny," she said, rolling her eyes at her big mouth best friend.

"What's good, Rose? You can call me Toflon."

"Un hum. Damn, a fine nigga with a sexy name like Toflon," Penny said with her hip poked out and a hand on her hip. Toflon could tell by the deep dark marks Penny hand on her knuckles, she was a fighter.

"Damn, you going to let me talk to him or you want to talk to him?" an aggravated Rose said.

"Oops, my bad, girl!" Penny said, stepping off and making her way inside of Amyir Jeweler's store. Rose couldn't believe how her friend just embarrassed her. She should be used to it though because Penny always seemed to find a way to embarrasses her with her ratchet ways.

"You have to excuse my girl. She has a tendency to speak whatever comes to her mind without even thinking." Rose blushed with humiliation.

"It's all good, beautiful. We all have friends like Penny," Toflon chuckled.

"See, if my man Butta was here, he would probably would have said out loud, 'Damn, Toflon. Shawty got a fat ass pussy print'," Toflon said in an animated voice like Butta's, while he dropped is eyes down to Rose's bulging crotch which made her giggle.

It also made her drop her perfect manicured hands in front of her private area. Rose wore a pair of white Seven jeans that showed off every curve. You could tell she didn't have on a stitch of fabric called panties on under the white jeans.

"Wow! He would have said all of that, huh?"

"Yup!" Toflon said with a smile on his face.

"Are you sure those are not your words and you're just using your boy as a way to tell me what you are thinking?" Rose said, smiling also. "Because if so, don't be afraid to say what's on your mind." Rose removed her hand from her crotch, letting Toflon get a full, uninterrupted view of her muffin print.

Toflon became aroused, invading Rose's personal space. She was standing so close to him that she could feel the hardness pressing against her leg. He whispered in her ear, "Beautiful Rose, if I had something to say, I wouldn't have a problem saying it. But since we are at the point of speaking our minds, I would like to take you out to dinner or a movie and then have a sweaty hot, ass-smacking, hair-pulling night of sex."

Rose started grinded up against Toflon, biting down on her bottom lip. "Well, since we're speaking our minds like you said, if your bank roll is as big as your dick, then we definitely can hang out." The woman that worked the pretzel stand had her face all balled up listening to them. At that moment, they were acting as if they were alone in the mall. Even though their meeting turned out to be a pay to play type of situation, they had an instant connection.

"Well, let me get your number and I'll give you a call."

Rose took two steps back and opened her Prada clutch purse, removing a pen and paper to write her digits down. As she did that, Toflon was examining her body. Her red skin was smooth with no blemishes. Her wide hips made him want to reach out and grab them just to see if they were real.

Rose stood about 5'7" with dark brown eyes and long, black hair that stretched down her back. She was mixed with something, but he couldn't with what at that particular time.

"Here you go, Mr. Toflon. I'll be waiting on your call," Rose said, passing her number to him. Toflon got caught staring at Rose's camel toe. He could see a small wet spot where her love box rested.

"My bad!" Toflon said, lifting his head as he brought his eyes up to meet hers. "Thanks. I—" He stopped as something behind Rose caught his attention. There stood Bear inside Aymir Jeweler's store speaking to a black Arab dude, but this wasn't your ordinary Arab.

This one right here had a little swag about himself. Toflon could tell by how he rocked his jeans and Timberlands with his all white T-shirt. He saw the Arab dude pass Bear a thick brown envelope. They tried to be discreet, but with Toflon being a jack boy and killer, he peeped the whole move. Bear and the Arab dapped each other up. Bear then saw Penny checking out some jewelry that was inside one of the display cases.

"Oh, let me find out since a price tag comes with this pussy, that you're not interested in me now and Penny is what you really want. I see you keep looking over my shoulder at her," Rose said with a little attitude.

"Naw, I just seen something," Toflon stated.

"I was getting ready to say because Penny is going to charge that ass, too. Why you think they call her Penny? She'll do anything for a pretty penny," Rose said, throwing shade on her friend. She was about to turn around to see what he was watching so intensely but he stopped her.

"Naw, ma. Don't turn around. Just keep talking to me," he said without taking his eyes off Bear and Penny. He was passing Penny his number. They engaged in a few more words before Bear made his way out the jewelry store. For some reason,

Toflon felt like something wasn't right. "Okay, Rose. I got to make some moves but I'll call you. Matter of fact, I'm going to call you and your girl. Here's some pocket change," Toflon said, reaching in the pocket of his jeans and removing $200.

"What's this for?" Rose asked, taking it.

"A hundred dollars for being beautiful and the other for your conversation." Toflon smiled and walked away with his bags and hot pretzels.

Chapter 25

Moe-B felt good being out of the county jail after two days. He swore the air on the outside of the jail smelled different from the inside. "You okay, baby?" Kay-Kay asked him from behind the driver's seat of her Honda Accord. Moe-B had his seat leaned all the way back as he enjoyed the high the kush gave him as he took another pull of the Atimo.

"Yeah, Kay. I'm good. Just can't wait to get to my uncle's house to get my strap. I feel naked without it," he said, taking another pull of the kush.

Kay just rolled her eyes, but she loved his gangsta. Kay and Moe-B's mother paid his bail yesterday. It took them all day to release him. By the time he was out, it was nine o'clock at night. Moe-B's mother refused to let him leave the house. That was fine with Kay-Kay because his mother allowed her to spend the night at her house with him. So, her and Moe-B showered and fucked most of the night.

She still could feel the soreness between her legs from where he hammered her pussy. Moe-B had to feeling her or he just plain old missed her because for the first time ever, he let her kiss him. "I hope you don't have any plans today because I'm going to need you to drive me around until I can get my car out the impound," he told her.

"I have no problem with that, love," she replied, turning up the radio when she heard Alicia Keys's song "Unthinkable" come on the radio.

Moe-B had some time to think while he sat in jail for the last past 48 hours. His mind often wondered back to his cousin Lil Tate. *How the fuck he going to have me kill my cousin, his nephew?* Moe-B thought to himself. *Then this nigga let BJ pull a burner on him and didn't even do shit about it, but had me kill my cuzzo for trying to rob BJ. Shit just not adding up.*

Today as he left his mom's house, she made a comment that had him tripping. "Don't you trust that black muthafucka. He don't give a shit about no one but himself." Moe-B didn't want to ask why his mother said that because Kay-Kay was with him. Still, he was aware his mother and uncle didn't see eye to eye for some reason. He wondered what he could have done to his mother that was so horrible.

"Baby, can we go to K. F. C when we leave here?" Kay-Kay asked, reaching over and touching Moe-B's thigh, breaking his train of thought.

"Um yeah, we can go grab something," he replied with slightly closed eyelids. The kush had him feeling good. Ten minutes later, they were pulling up in front of Homicide Jack's apartment building. "Listen, Kay-Kay. I'm going to run in here and holla at my uncle real quick. I'll be back in a minute." Moe-B leaned over and kissed her fully on her lips, adding a little tongue in the mix.

"Ok, Moe-B. I'll be here waiting," she said, watching him get out the car and walk up walkway to Homicide Jack's building. She instantly became mad at herself for sharing that sexual look with Moe-B's uncle yesterday.

Moe-B made his way to his uncle's door and knocked. He could hear rambling and moving around on the other side of the door. "Yo, who is it?"

Click, clack.

Moe-B could hear a gun being chambered through the door. "Aye, Unc. It's me, Moe-B. Open up, old head." He could hear the locks being popped on the door. Homicide opened the door without a shirt on. He carried a chrome pistol grip pump in his hand "What's good, Unc?" Moe-B said, stepping in the apartment and dapping his uncle up.

"I'm just laying low waiting to hear word from BJ. I'm glad they let your young ass out. What the fuck happened?" Homicide Jack questioned him as he closed the door behind him and locked it.

"Man, it's not much to tell, Unc. The police got behind me and I had to run them bitches. I had coke and two guns on me. I had too much shit on me to be pulled over. I hit Kay-Kay on the phone and put a plane together to get clean before the police boxed me in," he explained, sitting down in the recliner.

Homicide Jack just nodded his head up and down in agreement. Something looked odd about his eyes. He had a look that Moe-B had never seen before. He brushed it off as if the purp and Hennessey that sat on the table next to a Glock 17 had him looking crazy.

Homicide Jack laid the 12 gauge from the table and walked to his back room. He came back with the brown paper bag that Kay-Kay had given him, passing it to him.

"Good looking, Unc." Moe-B opened the bag and examined the contents. He stared at two ounces, his trusted .357 and the Smith and Western 45 that he took from Hammer.

Moe-B was puzzled as to why there was only two ounces in the bag instead on three. Then he thought that maybe his uncle used one of the ounces to get this bail money together with. He wasn't really tripping about the missing ounce. He was just happy to be out that stinking ass jail.

Moe-B took a deep breath before he asked his uncle the question he intended to ask him. "Unc, let me ask you a question." Moe-B fought to find the right words, but there were none. So, he just asked the question. "Why you had me kill Lil Tate? I mean at the end of the day, we was family."

His uncle looked at him, but the look was as if he was looking through him. "What the fuck? You getting soft on me, Moe-B?" he questioned his nephew.

"Naw, hell naw. It's nothing like that." Moe-B was now looking at his uncle sideways. It was as if he was trying to test his gangsta, questioning if he was getting soft.

"Huh? I can't tell. You in here questioning me about a nigga that betrayed us," Homicide stated as he grabbed the Hennessey off the table and drank from the bottle.

Moe-B wasn't feeling the way he was addressing him or the situation about Lil Tate. "Betrayed? Unc, Lil Tate didn't betray us. He betrayed BJ. He only did what you came up doing and that was taking other peoples' shit."

"No! Lil Tate was weak. He let others influence him to help Toflon take BJ's shit," Homicide Jack spat, raising his voice. "We work for BJ. He was supposed to be loyal to BJ. BJ put us on when we didn't have shit. Lil Tate was ungrateful just like his fucking mother," Homicide Jack said harshly.

"What! What the fuck you talking about, Unc? What you know about Auntie Rose?"

"Listen, Moe-B. In this game, you have to be strong as a bull in the midst of the storm. The rules of survival are set. You got to play by them. One of the rules is if a muthafucka crosses you, you make them pay." Homicide Jack then took another drink from the Hennessey bottle.

"Homicide, you talking in riddles. Spit that shit out. What the fuck you trying to say to me?" Moe-B said, getting agitated.

"Spell it out? You want me to spell it out? Okay, I will. I killed Rose and her punk ass boyfriend Trey. I gave that bitch a better life when she didn't have shit. She met that nigga Trey and fell in love with him. All she had to do was stick to the plan and set the nigga up like she did the rest of them niggas. But no, she went and switched the game up in the fourth quarter."

Moe-B's heart was racing. Homicide Jack, his uncle, had killed his own sister. "Lil Tate was just like his mother. He deserved to die just like his weak ass momma." Homicide Jack slammed the bottle of Hennessey down on the table, looking at his nephew. "I got it all spelled out for you, now what?" The thought crossed his mind right then and there that he might have to kill Homicide Jack. His uncle was only inches way from the Glock 17 and the pump shout gun. He knew he would have to go through too much to get one of the guns out the brown bag he had, so he played it smart about what he said out his mouth.

"Unc, everything is clear to me. I understand your action now. I'm hurt but the lessons we learn in life are sometimes hurtful. This lesson is a well taught one. I think that it hurt so bad because Tate was my cousin. I promise you don't never have to worry about me ever crossing you or questioning you again," Moe-B spoke calmly.

Homicide Jack studied him with a look in his eyes that was almost unreal. Moe-B felt uncomfortable.

"Look, Unc. I got Kay-Kay out in the car waiting on me, so let me get up outta here," Moe-B told him, easing to his feet. Homicide Jack slightly nodded his head.

"Yeah, you do that."

Moe-B made his way to the door. He could feel Homicide Jack's eyes on him. He unlocked the door and walked out, not looking back at his uncle. As soon as he got out, Moe-B placed the 45 on his hip and clutched the .357 Python in his hand underneath his shirt while he walked to the car. He got in the car stoned-faced. When he looked back at his uncle's apartment window, he could see him staring back at him through the blinds.

Chapter 26

The brimstone house in York Town County held a deadly silence. The house was so quiet, you could hear a mouse fart. Fever walked back and forth, staring into the eyes of every individual that occupied the room. His hand was tightly gripped around his 45.

"There's a muthafuckin' weak link amongst these racks. There's a bitch in here that wants me dead. Is it you?" Fever asked, pointing his gun at a freckle-faced dude by the name of Joker. Fever pressed the muzzle of his gun to Joker's chin. "Is it you, bitch?" Fever asked.

"Naw—Naw, Fever. You tripping, fam. I'm not on no bullshit like that," Joker stuttered with his words.

"Tripping? Tripping? A nigga in here trying to murder me and you tell me that I'm tripping? One of you niggas gave up my whereabouts and you say I'm tripping?" Fever paused and stared into the eyes of every individual in the room, while still holding the gun to Joker's chin. "You damn right I'm tripping," Fever said, pulling the trigger on the 45.

Boom!

The gun jumped hard in his hand. Immediately, the contents that only seconds ago occupied Joker's head, now rested on the faces and clothing of the people that were standing close to him. "Oh shit!" someone in the room yelled out after their shirt and face was plastered with blood and brain gook. The whole room got low, including Bear. The only person that held his composure was Toflon.

"Stand the fuck up!" Fever ordered the room. His people were hesitated getting to their feet, but they did except for one of his goons. He was balled up on the floor crying. "I said get your bitch ass up!" Fever yelled over the young goon's body.

James struggled to get to his feet with shaky legs. When he finally stood up, you could see a large wet spot that rested in the front of his pants. This enraged Fever. "You weak ass nigga. You let a loud noise and a little blood bring the bitch outta you?"

Boom! Boom!

Fever squeezed the 45 twice, knocking two holes in James's chest. He dropped to the floor, gasping for air. The gunpowder lingered in the air, lightly burning their eyes from him firing his gun in such close quarters. "I want to know who's working with Aymir. I want to know how Aymir's fake ass Arab muthafucka broke in and infiltrated my ranks. Those were his goons that came for me in Riley Circle projects," Fever said, forcefully sprinkling spit that flew out his mouth. His chest rose and fell. "I don't give a fuck if I got to kill every bitch in this muthafucka, I'm going find out who's committed this act of treason."

"Yo, Fever!" Toflon said, pushing up off the wall. Fever whipped around.

"What!" Fever said, gripping tightly to his 45.

Toflon walked over and whispered something in his ear. Fever immediately tucked his gun in the small of his back. "Aye Bear and Duck, clean his shit up. Nobody moves until this shit is cleaned up," Fever ordered before he headed towards the door with Toflon on his heels.

"Shit crazy out there. You should take me and Toflon with you," Bear stated.

"No, I need you here," Fever said as he exited the door with Toflon, leaving Bear puzzled.

***

"Shit, I got to get out this house. I need some fresh air and I need my hair done. I think I want to go to Heavenly Fashion salon," Vanessa spoke to herself. The thought of Heavenly Fashion made her think of 40, remembering it was no longer open due to his murder. They had so many good times at the both of his shops. She missed him so much. She couldn't believe BJ had her man killed like a dog. She wiped tears from her eyes.

She finished drying off, stepping into a pair of white and cranberry colored thongs. She walked over to the mirror and examined her war wounds on her chest. She was healing, but marks such as a scar from a bullet wound did something to a woman's mental. Vanessa did like she always did when she looked in the mirror at her scar. She traced it with her fingertips.

She rolled her eyes and put on her matching bra, exiting the bathroom as she headed to her room to find something to wear. Vanessa stopped by BJ's room first and entered his walk-in closet. She went to the safe that was concealed behind the clothes that were hung up. She bent over and twisted the dial on the safe, opening it.

Smack!

Vanessa jumped from being smack on the ass, throwing her hands up in a fighting position.

"Oh, baby. I'm sorry for scaring you," Moocha said, standing behind Vanessa with her hands up in the air in a surrendering position. Moocha's silk robe was opened, revealing her golden nipples and slightly shaved pussy.

"Moocha, you scared the fuck out of me!" she screamed, placing her hand over her chest.

"I'm sorry, mami," Moocha said, stepping close to her. She wrapped her arms around her and planted a kiss on her lips. Their tongues did their own dance, causing Vanessa to become wet. Moocha opened her eyes and peeked behind her as they remained in a lip lock.

"Damn, you really done saved up for a rainy day," Moocha said, pulling her lips away from Vanessa's. The safe was open, revealing stacks of money.

"Naw, that's not my money. That's BJ money, but we're going to spend some of it today," Vanessa told her, taking two large stacks of money out the safe and securing the door.

"So, you telling me that none of that money is yours?"

"Yup," Vanessa replied, looking puzzled.

"So what happens if the police came and raided the place and find the money? We both know BJ is out there in them streets doing everything under the sun. It's only going to be a matter of time before they get hip to him. Niggas in the streets turn state every day of the week. You got to have your own shit, Vanessa. Don't be like the rest of these dumb ass bitches waiting for the next nigga to take care of them," Moocha told her, speaking like she was coming straight from the heart.

"Damn, you sound just like my girl Trici with that speech," Vanessa replied. Her mind drifted back to the game that her friend tried to give her.

"Yeah, he looks out for me if you must know, but I have my own money and BJ does a good job of taking care of his big sister," Vanessa said, rolling her neck.

"What you mean he looks out for you? You call getting your nails and hair done looking out for you? Vanessa, you can get your own nails and hair done," Trici said, trying to make something out of nothing with her conversation. "You don't want your own money? You ever thought about being independent where you don't have to depend on a nigga or your brother to take care of you?" Trici asked her.

"Yeah, who wouldn't want to be free of not having to depend on someone?" Vanessa replied, sealing another crack bag.

"Girl, I'm going to have my own money, even if I got to get it the grimy way," Trici spoke with a hint of serious in her voice.

"Vanessa! Vanessa!" Moocha said in her face, shaking her.

"I want my own money," Vanessa blurted out loud, snapping out of her trip down memory lane.

"Ok, mami. We can work on that, but where the fuck you just went on me? You just zoned out on me, mami," she questioned Vanessa, staring at her like maybe she losing her mind.

"I was thinking about my friend Trici. She told me the same shit you're telling me about having my own money."

"Where is this Trici? I like her already," Moocha probed.

"She got murdered." Vanessa's eyes became misty, thinking about her friend, another loved one that BJ had murdered.

Moocha's hand flew to her mouth. "Fucking loco," Moocha mumbled, wrapping Vanessa in her arms. "Damn, Vanessa. I'm sorry. Your brother is killing everyone that loves you," Mooch whispered in her ear as she held her.

"It seems like that Moocha. I hate BJ. I'm going to make him pay. I'm going to make him pay for Rob and Trici," she told her.

Chapter 27

"Man, this is some fucked up shit here. The bastard killed the poor girl's mother and father right in front of her," Detective Tillman said to his partner.

"What do you expect out these fuckers in this city they are straight monsters?" Detective Thomas responded nonchalantly. They walked down the hallway towards the officer's lounge where their only witness to the double homicide case had just been assigned to them.

For some reason, Detective Tillman knew that this case was going to have a major effect over him. They always do when there is a child involved. They walked into the lounge and saw a pretty little girl talking to a Department of Social Services worker. The little girl looked frail and scared. She held a Dora Explorer doll on her lap. Her braided hair was fuzzy. She twirled the doll's arm slowly back and forth, not out of anger but more out of nervousness from being in the company of people she didn't know. The social worker contacted the girl's grandparents who were on their way up from South Carolina.

"Hello, young lady! I'm Detective Tillman and this big ole guy right here is my friend, Detective Thomas." The little girl looked up from twisting her doll's arm and placed her sad eyes on Detective Tillman and his partner.

Detective Tillman almost broke down when he peered into the girl's eyes. He could tell she had seen something that a 7-year-old should never have to see. Detective Thomas knew this drill too well. He went straight to the vending machine. He purchased snacks and sodas, bringing the items back to where the fragile witness sat with the social worker at the round table.

"What's your name, beautiful?" Detective Thomas asked although he already knew the girl's name. He'd been briefed when they called him in on the case. They advised him that Layla had been hiding under the bed for two days with her deceased mother and father lying dead on the living room floor.

The next-door neighbor came over to borrow some sugar. She found the door unlocked and what she found on the other side of the door would haunt her forever. There were two decomposed bodies. The neighbor screamed out and fled the apartment.

Later when the police arrived on the scene, they found a hungry and scared Layla. She was hiding under her bed holding a Dora the Explorer doll and a picture frame.

"Layla," the little girl said, not looking at Detective Tillman.

"Would you like a soda, chips, cookies or candy bar?" he asked, trying to get Layla as comfortable as possible so she would talk to him. She nodded her head up and down. Detective Tillman pushed a grape soda and a bag of bar-b-que chips in front of the little girl. She immediately went for the grape soda. Detective Tillman opened the soda for her, watching Layla drank her fill. Next, she went to the chips.

"How old are you, Layla?"

"I'm seven and a half," Layla said, talking with her mouth full.

"Wow! Seven and a half. What grade are you in?" Detective Tillman asked.

"Second grade. Mrs. Barns is my teacher."

"Ok, what school do you go to?" he asked while he took notes.

"Ummm, Mercury Elementary," Layla replied, taking another sip of her grape soda.

"Okay, that's a nice school," Detective Tillman told her, smiling at Layla. "Layla, can you tell me and my partner what happened to your mommy and daddy?" The little girl stopped chewing, closing her eyes tightly.

"It's okay, Layla. I know that it's painful but you have to tell Detective Tillman. No one is going to hurt you." The social worker safely placed a tender hand on Layla's small arm. Her heart went out to this poor child. She just hoped that the grandparents could give her all the love she needed to get over this traumatic event.

"You pinky swear?" Layla whispered.

"Of course, I promise," the social worker, said hugging Layla while making eye contact with the detectives.

"Layla, we all promise you that no one will hurt you if you tell us what happened to your mommy and daddy," Detective Tillman said, trying to bring some reassurance to the young child. What happened next scared him. Layla's slanted her eyes in a demonic way, while pointing her hand at Detective Tillman in a gun-like figure and said, "Bang, bang, bang."

The act was horrifying, but it did confirm that Layla had witnessed the demise of her parents. The social worker swallowed hard. The detectives were stuck in their own thoughts, Detective Tillman being the first to recover.

"Layla, who went 'bang, bang, bang'?" he asked, not really thinking she could answer the question but that was the first one that entered his mind after Layla shot him with her finger pointing gun.

"My Uncle Toflon," Layla said in lowly. She put her grape soda can on the table and started back twisting her doll's arm.

"Your Uncle Toflon?" Detective Tillman stated, jumping into the interview. Layla moved her head up and down. She reached behind her back, pulling a small, framed picture out and said, "See me, mommy, daddy and Uncle Toflon at my birthday party?"

Detective Tillman leaned over the table to look at the picture she held in her hand. Sure enough, it was a picture of a smiling Layla wearing a cone birthday hat with her deceased parents and Uncle Toflon standing behind them, wearing a wicked smile that exposed the gap between his two front teeth.

Chapter 28

"Come on, man. I was going to pay, Slim. I swear I was," the fat dude cried, clutching the bullet wound in his leg. LJ stood over of him with a smoking 9-millmeter equipped with a silencer.

Phuff!

The gun in LJ's hand barely made a sound. The fat dude screamed out, feeling the hot copper penetrate his kneecap shattering his bones.

"Where the money at? If you tell me where the money at, you'll live to see another day," LJ said.

"It's—it's in the mattress," the fat dude managed to say through the pain.

Phuff!

The 9-millimeter released out another round into LJ's captive, causing him greater pain then the first bullet he'd just received.

"Arrrrggghh! Arrrggghh! Come on, man. I just told you where the money was," Fatso cried out with tears and snot running out his nose.

"If you muthafuckas would pay your fucking debts, you won't have to worry about seeing me," LJ said, snatching the dingy sheet off the bed and cutting the seam of the mattress.

And just like the fat boy said, the money was inside the mattress. LJ opened the plastic, confirming if it was actually money in the bag. It looked to be about twenty thousand dollars in the bag. He shook his head in disgrace. This nigga owed Slim seventy-five thousand dollars and all he had was twenty thousand.

Slim hired him to find the chump and locate his money. If he had all the money, he had orders to let the dude live but if he didn't, he was to kill him. LJ looked at the fat boy trembling on the floor crying like a bitch. He walked past him and out the door. The fat boy thought it was all over until LJ reappeared in the doorway, squeezing three shots in his face.

Phuff! Phuff! Phuff!

***

"Oh shit! Oh shit!" Kay-Kay yelled as Moe-B pounded into her like he was mad at the world.

He had her ankles pinned down by her ears as he pounded away. Kay-Kay could tell he was nowhere near cumming. They'd been going at it for the last 45 minutes. Her right leg was becoming numb. "Come on, Moe-B. Cum for me. Cum for Kay-Kay," she begged him, trying to coach him to a orgasm, but it wasn't working.

Ever since the night Moe-B left his uncle's apartment, he'd been in a strange mood. All he did was smoke, drink, and fuck Kay-Kay's brains out. He fucked her in every hole. She was sore and her jaws had locked up on her twice that day. Kay-Kay looked up into Moe-B eyes as if he was in another world. Sweat dripped off his chest on to her. "No, stop! Stop! Moe-B, stop!" Kay-Kay screamed out.

"What?" Moe-B replied, snapping out of his trance, still having Kay-Kay ankles pinned by her ears.

"You hurting me, Moe-B. Give me a break." Kay-Kay had tears in her eyes. Moe-B's manhood gave off a wet slurpy sound as he pulled out of her. He rolled over on his back, lying next to Kay-Kay as he breathed hard. He grabbed the blunt off the nightstand next to the bed and lit it up.

"Damn. My bad, Kay-Kay," he said, taking a deep pull of the blunt.

"Moe-B, what's wrong with you?" Kay-Kay rolled over on her side and faced her lover. Moe-B let the kush seep out his nose as he stared at the ceiling.

"Nothing, Kay-Kay."

"I can't tell it's nothing because you've been taking out all of your frustration on my pussy," she told him, hitting Moe-B playfully in the arm.

"I'm sorry about that. I just found some shit out about my uncle that made me look at him in a different light, that's all."

"Well, it must be serious because I even heard you crying in your sleep last night," Kay-Kay said, touching Moe-B's stomach.

"Shawty, you got me fucked up. You ain't never heard or seen me cry." Moe-B was mad and embarrassed. He quickly sat up and planted his bare feet on the floor. Kay-Kay crawled behind him, placing her bare breasts on his back as she wrapped her arms and legs around him.

"Everyone cries, Moe-B. Men cry, thugs cry. Crying is nothing to be ashamed of. It shows that you are human. It confirms that you have a heart and that you are capable of being loved," Kay-Kay said, placing a kiss on his back.

Moe-B was mentally crushed to learn that his uncle, Homicide Jack, his hero, had killed Lil Tate's mother, which was his uncle's sister. With the tension in the room that night, Moe-B knew his uncle was thinking about grabbing that 12 gauge off the table and ending his life. Kay-Kay tightly squeezed her legs and arms around her lover. Moe-B rubbed her thighs, taking a pull of the blunt before he passed it back to Kay-Kay.

"Kay-Kay?"

"Yeah, baby?" she replied in between pulls of the blunt.

"You love me?" Moe-B asked. Kay-Kay unwrapped her legs and got out of bed. She then stood in front of him, placing her slightly shaved and swollen vagina in his face.

"Yes, baby. You know that I love you." Kay-Kay lifted his face up by his chin so he could look dead into her eyes and see the sincerity in them.

"Good. From now on, never trust my uncle. Never trust him around me or yourself. When it comes to him, I need you to be the eyes in the back of my head," Moe B told her with sadness in his voice.

"I got you, boo," she said, pushing him back on the bed and placing his manhood in the back of her throat.

Chapter 29

Tashia drove her Benz truck with ease as BJ sat on the passenger seat enjoying a blunt of purp as he talked on his phone. She felt like she was in heaven, spending the last three days with BJ uninterrupted and without limits. She really felt the difference between being a hustler's wife and a plain old wife. If asked, she would easily choose on any given day to just be a regular wife, to be able to walk through the National Aquarium and the National Zoo, holding hands with BJ. To her, that would be magnificent. She peeked over at her future husband with his fitted cap pulled low over his eyes.

Damn, my baby is sexy as hell, she said to herself. BJ peeped her watching him, blowing her a kiss as he continued to talk on the phone. She hated returning to Newport News. She wished she could have stayed at the "W" in DC with BJ for another three days. She pulled into the parking lot of MacArthur Mall.

"Yeah, Papi. Everything is good. I just had to lie low for a minute to see what was what and who was who. I see Bugg has been one of the loyal ones," BJ spoke through the phone. "Yeah. Okay, next week," he said, disconnecting the call with his connect. He had to break everything down to him about being questioned by the police.

BJ dialed Homicide Jack's number but he got no answer. He found that kind of odd because Homicide Jack always answered his phone whenever he called. So, he dialed Moe-B's number who picked up on the fourth ring.

"Speak to me!" Moe-B said in a cool, calm, and collective voice.

"Is everything alright?" BJ asked. Moe-B recognized his voice, bringing him out of that cool, calm, and collective state.

"Oh shit! When you get out, nigga?" Moe-B asked excitedly.

"A few hours ago," BJ lied.

"Damn, where you at, BJ?"

"Right now, I'm just pulling up at the mall. Tashia insisted she bring me through to cop me a few outfits."

"That's what's up. Oh, you heard what happened around Riley Circle?" Moe-B asked him.

"Naw, lace me up about it," BJ replied.

"Man, them muthafuckas had a major shoot out. Man, they had muthafuckas hanging out of widows in the projects busting machine guns and all type of shit," Moe-B said excitedly.

"Oh yeah? But what's going on with the business though?" BJ asked him, changing the subject as he brushed off Moe-B's comments about the shootout off.

"Umm, everything good but we had a minor setback."

"What's the minor setback?" BJ asked in a serious tone.

"I had to take them local boys on a run. I ended up spending two days in the county, but I was on the juvenile side though."

"What did they catch you with?" BJ asked in concern.

"They didn't catch me with shit. I got a chance to toss the two ounces I had on me," Moe-B replied.

"Alright, that's good. But that's the shit you should have been telling me at first instead of some fucking shoot out in projects," BJ said, getting a little angry.

"My bad, fam."

"Yeah, your bad, but where' s Homicide Jack? I've been trying to get in touch with him."

"Man, I don't even know. He hasn't been answering his phone," Moe-B said nonchalantly.

"Damn, I just called him and his phone went to voicemail after five rings. Listen, go past his apartment and if you don't get a hold of him, then go through and holla at Channtel to see if he's there. If he's not, then hit me up. But if you locate him, tell him to check in with me ASAP!"

Moe-B pulled the phone away from his ear, looking at it like he had a venomous snake in his hand. He wasn't feeling how BJ was bossing him around. "A'ight, I'm on it," he replied after placing the phone back to his ear.

"A'ight then, handle that and get back with me," BJ said, ending the call and putting his phone in his pocket. He got out the SUV. Then, he and Tashia walked into the mall, heading straight to Aymir's Jeweler store. When BJ entered the stored, he saw a familiar face.

"Hello, Mr. BJ," the sales clerk said, remembering his name.

"What's up, Brenda," BJ said, greeting the woman with a handshake. "And this is that special lady I came to buy that engagement ring for a few months ago," he said, smiling.

"Hi!" Tashia said with a smile, flashing her two and half diamond karat ring.

"Hello to you and for the record, I love that ring," Brenda, the sales woman said, matching Tashia's smile.

"Is Aymir in?" BJ asked.

"Yes, let me get him for you," Brenda replied. She went behind the display case picking up the phone to speak to him. Moments later, a militant looking guy came out the back. He took post by the door same he'd just walked out of. A few seconds later, Aymir came out. He was decked out in his usual attire, a pair of blue jeans, a crisp all white T-shirt and some fresh Air Force One's, rocking no jewels.

"My man, BJ. How you doing? It's been a minute," Aymir said, extending his hand for a handshake, which BJ gladly accepted.

"What's good, Aymir? You know me, trying to make moves and stay out the way."

"That's the best way to be," Aymir replied. What can I do for you?"

"Ummm!" BJ said, digging in his pocket. He removed the damaged Jesus piece, handing it to Aymir. Aymir turned the piece over in his hand and inspected it thoroughly.

"Damn, I've seen this piece before. Matter of fact, I've done work on this piece before. I upgraded this. Look, every jeweler has their own signature markings they place on the jewelry they worked on," he said, still eyeing the Jesus piece.

"This piece was brought into my other location at Patrick Henry Mall. A guy named Block brought this in for a upgrade."

"Damn, small fucking world. Block was my man," BJ lied. "Before he died, he gave my sister this chain. My sister got shot and this Jesus piece saved her life. The bullet struck the Jesus piece instead of my sister's chest. That's why it's damaged the way it is."

"What a fucking story!" Aymir said in amazement.

Tashia just stood there amazed that BJ personally knew a real jeweler. She was more amazed, however, how his ass told that bold face lie without blinking an eye. *I'm going to have to watch his slick ass*, she thought to herself.

"Yeah, that's why I'm here. I want to have this piece repaired or melted down and remade," BJ said.

"I think that I can handle that. I would have to melt it down and remake the piece," Aymir replied.

"Ok, that would be great!" said BJ. He wanted to do something for his sister.

He knew they were at odds about his decision to have 40 killed. He just hoped that by him replacing the chain that saved her life, would be symbolic of him waving the peace flag. "So, what's the price tag to do this?" BJ asked.

"Well, just step in the back and we can talk about it. I got some news that you would like to hear anyway," Aymir said, leading the way to his office in the back of the store. "Oh, Brenda. Help Tashia select a nice tennis bracelet of her liking. It's in the house," Aymir instructed her over his shoulder.

Tashia looked at BJ for approval. He just shrugged his shoulders, following Aymir into the back room. Aymir took a seat behind his desk and retrieved a blunt from his desk drawer. He lit the blunt and inhaled deeply. BJ took a seat in front of his desk.

The militant looking dude stood post by the door. "Excuse me, Eric. I need to have a minute alone," Aymir said to his bodyguard. He nodded his head and stepped out of the office, closing the door behind him. Aymir didn't waste any time getting down to business.

"Do you know a nigga named Fever that sells a large amount of purp in the city?" Aymir asked as he took a another pull from the blunt.

"Naw, I can't say for sure that I know him, but the name does ring a bell though," BJ replied, wondering where this conversation was headed.

"Ok, what about Toflon?" Aymir asked, staring into BJ's eyes. BJ sat up in his chair.

"Yeah, I know Toflon. What about him though?" BJ replied, asking a question of his own.

"I can provide you with the info you need to handle your beef with Toflon."

"How the fuck you know about my business with Toflon?" BJ asked sternly.

"I got an inside source in Fever's camp that tells me that you got beef with Toflon."

"Ok, I get it. I'm from the streets and the streets have taught me that nothing is free, so what's your stake in this for you to telling me?" Aymir liked how BJ thought on his toes.

"Well, it's simple. When you hit Toflon, I want Fever taken out also," Aymir said with a slight grin on his face.

"I'm not a hired gun. Why you can't handle your own situation you got going on with Fever?" BJ questioned.

"I tried but shit got way out of hand in Riley Circle."

"That was you?" BJ asked, remembering what Moe-B told him earlier about the shooting. Aymir just nodded his head up and down.

"Shit hot for me, BJ. I'm a businessman. War and money don't mix, but I got a deal for you. If you make the hit for me, there'll be two hundred and fifty thousand dollars in it for you and I'll become your plug. I'll supply you enough purp to supply the people from South Carolina all the way to DC." BJ was working the math in his head and all he could come up with is millions. He knew this was a plug of a lifetime.

"Listen, Aymir. Let me think about this and I'll get back with you in a few days," BJ said, standing up.

"BJ, I got intel where Toflon and Fever are going to be at the same time. All you have to do is just be there and do your thing," Aymir said, making a gun with his hand and pulling the trigger. BJ knew shit was never that easy.

"Like I said, Aymir. Let me think about it. Now, how much for the Jesus piece?"

"It's on the house," Aymir said, standing to his feet to give BJ a pound. He then exited the office with a lot on his mind.

Chapter 30

The black Dodge Magnum followed the Benz truck out of the MacArthur Mall's parking lot. His black leather gloves tightly gripped the steering wheel. He'd been watching BJ ever since him and Tashia left to go on their mini vacation in DC. He was hoping to get an opportunity to hit BJ in DC, but they never really left the downtown area.

The presence of law enforcements was heavy in the downtown area and the "W" hotel wasn't any better. The security was tighter than a turtle's pussy due to hotel hosting several high-profiled celebrities. The Dodge Magnum let three cars get in between him and BJ. He was stalking BJ like a snake stalks its prey, waiting for the right time to strike.

***

"Baby, your friend Aymir really showed me some love on this tennis bracelet," Tashia said with her wrist extended out, profiling her newest edition of jewelry. She couldn't believe Aymir just up and gave her a diamond tennis bracelet of her choice. "Baby, you're the man! Got jewelers giving your wife diamonds for free!" Tashia said, smiling.

"Oh, nothing is free," BJ mumbled under his breath. He knew Aymir had a motive for giving Tashia the tennis bracelet, just like Aymir didn't charge him anything to rebuild the Jesus piece. Tashia turned in her seat and faced him with her face scrunched up.

"I heard that, BJ! What you mean by that? I mean, I don't even know Aymir. What's up with that slick ass comment?" she asked.

"I didn't mean nothing by it, Tashia. Just let it go. I got other shit on my mental right now," BJ said, stopping at a red light.

"Yeah, I bet you do have a lot on you mind, but if you're that insecure about this punk ass bracelet, then I'll take it off," she said, unhooking the bracelet. BJ stopped her.

"You should know that a nigga is never insecure about nothing. You're my wifey. Ain't nothing ever coming in between us. No bitch, no nigga, no money and especially no punk ass jewelry. Now, keep the bracelet on. That shit looks hot on you," BJ said with a smile on his face. Tashia leaned over and kissed him on his cheek.

"I love you, Bryant," Tashia in between kisses.

"I know you do, baby!"

Beep! Beep! Beep!

The horn blared behind BJ, letting him know that his intimate moment was over with. He hit the gas and drove through the light.

Ring! Ring!"

BJ's phone could be heard ringing from his front pocket. *This must be Homicide Jack or Moe*-B, BJ thought. Looking at his screen, he saw it was Vanessa. He smiled knowing his big sister would finally come to her senses about the decision he had to make about 40. "Hey, sis. What's good?" he asked, placing the phone on speaker. All he could hear was her crying. Panic immediately set in. "Hello! Hello, Vanessa? What's going on, sis?"

"Th—they took everything. They robbed me, BJ," Vanessa cried through the phone.

"What! Who did what?"

"They robbed the house, BJ. They took all the money!"

"I'm on my way, Vanessa. Just hold tight, sis," BJ said, disconnecting the call and pressing down hard on the accelerator. He passed Tashia the phone. "Get Moe-B on the line. Tell him to get to Vanessa's house ASAP. Then get a hold of Homicide Jack and tell him the same thing." Tashia followed her hubby's orders. She couldn't get a hold of Homicide Jack, but she left a message on his voicemail.

"Bitch!" BJ yelled out as he zigzagged through traffic, racing to get to her house. He was thinking about all the money he had stashed at her house. "Fuck!" he yelled again. His driving was scaring Tashia as she put her seat belt on.

"Baby, can you please slow down?" she begged, but he ignored her. Fifteen minutes later, BJ turned down the block where Vanessa lived. From the outside, everything looked peaceful. He pulled into the driveway and jumped out the truck, racing into the house.

Tashia was on his heels, seeing a strange dark-colored Dodge Magnum bend the corner. She continued to follow behind BJ. As they entered the house, they saw Vanessa sitting and holding an ice pack over her eye. Her bottom lip was cut too. Seeing BJ, Vanessa ran and jumped in her brother's arms as she cried her heart out. BJ held his sister tightly. Tashia stood behind him, taking in her surroundings. Something just didn't sit right with her about this. *And where the fuck was Moocha,* she wondered to herself.

"Let me look at you," BJ said to his sister, pushing her away then examining her face. He could see the fresh swelling around her eye. It was already turning black.

He traced his thumb over her split lip. "What happened?" he asked. Vanessa took a seat back on the sofa, returning the ice pack back over her eye.

"I was on my way to the store. When I opened the door, there was this guy just standing there. He hit me in the eye and I fell to the floor," Vanessa said through tears. "He came into the house with a gun. He pointed the gun at my head then asked me where the money was. I told him there was no money in here. He then backhanded me in my mouth. I was so scared, BJ. I had to take him to the safe. I gave him the money and he left," she said, staring down at a stain that was on the carpet.

Tashia turned Vanessa's story over and over in her head. Something didn't set well with her about her story.

"What the dude look like, Vanessa?" BJ inquired, taking a knee in front of her to look her in her face. Vanessa paused.

"It was that dude you had problems with at the club on your birthday."

"Toflon! That bitch ass nigga did this?" BJ yelled.

He was enraged Toflon violated his sister's house and stole his money. Out of instinct, Tashia peeked out the window and saw the black Dodge Magnum sitting across the street from the house. She couldn't see who was in the car, but she could tell someone was. BJ went to check the safe and it was empty. Tashia went and looked around the house, seeing everything was intact.

"Aye, BJ!" Moe-B called out from the living room. When BJ entered the living room, he could see murder on his face. "What's good, fam?" he asked with concern in his voice.

"The nigga, Toflon! That's what's up. That nigga hit my safe!"

"Daaaamn! Fam, we got to body this nigga. He's living way longer then he's supposed to. Why haven't you put that hired gun on him the same one you put one on 40?" BJ and Tashia both regretted the words they heard coming out of Moe-B's mouth. They both looked at Vanessa who continued to hold the ice pack to her face, not saying a word about what Moe-B just said.

"Listen, Vanessa. Go in the room and lay down. I'll be in there in a minute to check up on you," Tashia told her. Vanessa didn't hesitate to leave the room. You could tell that she was bothered by what Moe-B said.

"Naw, Moe-B. I got to handle this myself. This is personal. This nigga kills my mom, then he robs me? Fuck that. I'm hitting his ass myself. I'm going to be the nigga behind the gun on this," BJ said, gritting his teeth.

"I can respect that, fam but we need to get a handle on this shit."

Knock! Knock!

They heard the knock at the door, interrupting their conversation. BJ looked though the peephole. Homicide Jack was standing on the other side of the door. BJ let him in. He wasn't familiar with the Homicide Jack that walked through the door, neither was Moe-B. Homicide Jack's clothes were dirty and wrinkled. If was as if he hadn't changed them in days. His bald head and face needed a shave.

"What's good, young blood?" Homicide Jack said, giving BJ some dap and Tashia a light hug. Tashia had to hold her breath. He was musty as hell. He smelled like the onions, the ones you put on your hog dogs at one of a hot dog stands.

"That nigga Toflon robbed me, old head. He got me for about two hundred and ten thousand dollars."

"Damn, fam. That's a lot of bread," Moe-B said, BJ and Homicide Jack ignoring his comment.

"So, what's the game plan, young blood?"

"I got some information about that nigga Toflon today. Let me look into some shit and I'll bring you the details and the plan. Until then, we need to grind harder. Go back and open the old trap house up on twenty-fourth street. Moe-B, I don't want you in that trap house. Hire someone to work the spot," BJ instructed.

"I hear you, fam but are you sure about that?" Moe-B questioned.

"Yeah, without a doubt. I'm going to hit you all up in three days for a meeting. Until then, grind hard and keep an eye open for that nigga Toflon," BJ stated, giving Homicide and Moe-B some dap as he dismissed them.

Tashia stood at the window watching the black Dodge Magnum pull away from in front of the house once Moe-B and Homicide Jack exited.

"Baby, there was a black Dodge Magnum sitting outside the house. When we first got here, I saw that same car turn the corner behind us. I didn't think nothing of it, but that may have been Toflon in that black Magnum," she told him.

"Why didn't you say something earlier? I could have—"

"Done what? Run out there and killed him in front of the house?" Tashia yelled, interrupting his statement with logic. BJ wanted to be mad, but he understood where she was coming from. He sat down on the sofa in frustration, placing his face in the palms of his hands.

Vanessa came out the backroom with an overnight bag draped over her shoulders. “Where you going?” BJ asked.

“I’m going to stay over at Moocha’s place until I feel comfortable enough to come back here. But right now, I just can’t stay here,” she sadly admitted.

“Nessa, you’re always welcomed to come stay with me and Tashia. You don’t have to stay with a stranger,” BJ told her.

“I’m fine staying with Moocha and she’s not a stranger,” Vanessa responded, checking BJ. He was getting ready to protest, but Tashia shook her head left to right. She noticed how Vanessa went from crying hysterically to becoming angry.

“Ok, do you need some money?” BJ asked, reaching in his pocket and removing a large knot of money.

“Bruh, I don’t need anything from you I got my own money,” Vanessa stated. She grabbed her car keys of the table and exited the house, leaving BJ and Tashia looking confused.

Chapter 31

"Okay, Thomas. We just got the warrant signed by Judge Bailey to arrest Tony 'Toflon' Mets," Detective Tillman said to his partner as he walked through the office door, grabbing his suit jacket off the back of the chair. "It was hard to convince the judge to issue a warrant even though Layla was an eye witness to the murder. Especially because of her age and the fact she could have suffered traumatically after seeing her parents' murder. But once the neighbor across the hall came forward and told detectives she saw Toflon leaving after hearing gunshots, the warrant was signed. She even gave up Toflon's real name. She knew it after doing Pookie a favor, bailing Toflon out of jail. He paid her the money to do it."

"It's about fucking time. I can't wait to slap my chuffs on his ass," Detective Thomas stated with malice in his voice. He stood to his feet, checking his 9-millimeter out to make sure he had one in his chamber.

"I got a team downstairs now preparing to assist us with executing the warrant at Toflon's last known address," Detective Tillman said, checking his side arm also.

***

"Fuck! Moocha, you didn't have to hit me that damn hard. Look at my eye. You hit me like you was mad at me or something," Vanessa complained, checking her busted eye in the mirror.

"I'm sorry, but I had to make it look real and believable." Moocha walked up behind Vanessa, kissing her on the neck and wrapping her arms around her waist. "Do you think BJ suspects anything?" she asked.

"Hell no! You should have seen me," Vanessa boasted. I should have gotten an Oscar for that award-winning performance. I was crying and trembling like a fearful puppy." Moocha smiled at her lover

"That's good to hear, girl. But you can never be too careful because niggas out there in them streets kill about their money. They don't care if you are family or not," Moocha stated seriously.

"How much did we get?" Vanessa asked, brushing off Moocha's statement.

"One hundred and fifty thousand."

"One hundred and fifty thousand? My brother said it was two hundred and ten thousand. Where the other sixty thousand went?" Vanessa asked, facing Moocha.

"Oh, that's my cut. I hope you didn't think I didn't deserve a cut? I mean I did help plan this right along with you," Moocha said. She looked Vanessa in the eyes, trying to figure out if she was going to have to double cross her down the line.

"No, girl. It's not like that. I was just wondering," Vanessa said, kissing Moocha tempestuously. She returned the kiss with the same amount of compassion.

"Let me make you cum all over that money," Moocha suggested, pointing to the bed covered with the money

"It would be my pleasure," Vanessa replied. She stripped down to her birthday suit, lying naked on top of the money. She opened her legs wide, telling Moocha to come and get it.

***

Off Mercury Boulevard behind the Coliseum Mall, both detectives and a six other warrant-serving officers stood gathered behind a moving truck on the opposite side of the street. They had a clear view of the rundown house, which was Toflon's last known address. The house was owned by a Chuck Mets. On file, he was Toflon's grandfather.

"Okay, gentlemen. You all knew the drill. We hit the house fast and hard. Keep our heads down and watch each other's' backs," Detective Tillman said. "Okay, Thomas. You take your team and hit the back. I'll take my team and hit the front. We breach both doors at the same time. Everything is on my call," Detective Tillman said. All them nodded their heads in agreement.

As the officers left to get in their positions, a light drizzle started to fall. Detective Tillman hated to work in the rain. He led his team to the front door of the weary looking house. "Team B, this is Team A. Are you in position?" he asked through his earpiece.

"That's a 10-4 on your call, sir!" Detective Thomas replied back.

Detective Tillman took a deep breath and announced, "All units move in." Detective Tillman banged on the door three times and shouted, "Police, search warrant! He stepped to the side, letting an officer that was waiting with battle ram knock the door off its hinges with swiftness. Once opened, the officers rushed the house.

Team A and B met up in the living room after finding the kitchen and living empty. They headed to the stairs that led up to the second level of the house. Midway up the stairs, a tall dark figure emerged from one of the rooms on the right.

Pop! Pop! Pop! Pop! Pop! Pop!

The figure's M16 tore holes in the wooden staircase, sending the officers diving back down the stairs and over the rails as they tried to save their lives. Detective Tillman returned fire.

Boom! Boom!

The figure ducked back off into the room.

Boom! Boom! Boom!

Detective Tillman and the rest of the officers started shooting wildly.

Boom! Boom! Boom! Bong! Bong! Bong!

At the top of the stairs, it was pitched black. One of the officers was lying on the side, clutching on as blood poured through his fingers. An M16 round found a home there. The officers struggled to recover. One officer screamed into his walkie talkie, "Shots fired! Officer down! We need back up at 1957 Park Street." The M16 opened up again.

Pop! Pop! Pop! Pop! Pop! Pop! Pop!

The officer return fired.

Boom! Boom! Boom! Boom! Boom! Boom!

"Hey, Tillman! I think he's reloading! Cover me," the young officer said as he took off up the flight of stairs.

"No!" Detective Tillman screamed out. He had no choice but to blindly shoot up the stairs, providing the rookie some cover fire.

Boom! Boom! Boom!

The Rookie made it up the stairs without getting shot. Tillman was relieved but he knew the lad wasn't out of danger yet. The rookie hugged the walls of the hallway. His heart was racing in his chest. It was so dark that he could barely see. The rookie heard something coming from one of the rooms on the right side of the hallway. He focused on the noise as he eased by the opened doorway on his left. He'd made up his mind that once the gunman showed himself on the right, he would kill him. The rookie froze in his tracks once he felt the barrel of the M16 pressed against his ear.

"Drop the gun, Vecon," the gunman whispered.

"Get the hell out my house!" a woman in the flower hat said. Out of reflex, the officers turned around and opened fire without thinking, full of fear.

"Nooooo!" Detective Thomas yelled out, but it was too late. He watched flashes jump from his fellow officers' guns.

Boom! Boom! Boom! Boom! Boom! Boom!

Everything went in slow motion. The flower hat the woman was wearing popped off her head as the bag of groceries fell from her hands. Her fragile old body collapsed and folded like a lawn chair. One shot to her head and two to shots hit her center mass in the chest, left her silent as she bled out. She died before she even before hit the floor.

The gunman heard his wife's voice, making him stop in mid-stride. The gun shots and the shouting of someone saying "no" made him grip the M16 tighter. His voice cracked. "Move! Let's go."

The rookie was surprised the gunman wasn't leading him further into the house. He was relieved he was being taken back downstairs. They reached the lip of the stairs and the board creaked.

"Gun!" an officer shouted. All officers trained their weapons on the suspect now standing at the top of the stairs with one of their very own held hostages. He held a military weapon to the back of his head.

The gunman took the night vision goggles off. He stood at the top of the stairs in a pair of boots, a Vietnam helmet, and wearing a pair of tighty whiteys as he held an M16.

"Sir, drop your weapon," Detective Thomas ordered. He clearly could see the gunman was an old man. *This must be Toflon's grandfather*, Thomas thought.

"Mr. Chuck Mets, please drop your weapon!" Detective Thomas shouted again. For a moment, it looked like he was going to comply until he saw his wife laid spread eagle on the floor. Her best Sunday's dress was up, exposing her white-laced grannie panties in a puddle of blood.

"You killed her!" Mr. Met's voice quivered, while still holding the M16 to the back of the rookie's head. "You fucking Vecons killed my Betty Sue!" Two solid tears fell from the old man's eyes.

"Hold up! Mr. Mets, we can fix this! We can fix this!" Detective Tillman said, pointing at Mr. Mets' dead wife.

"Fuck you! This is a good day to die and kill some Vecons! I'm coming Betty Sue! I'm coming!" he yelled, squeezing the trigger of the M16.

Pop!

The back of the rookie's cranium exploded, jumping out front and sending the rookie tumbling down the stairs. Mr. Mets came right behind him firing his M16.

Pop! Pop! Pop! Pop! Pop!

Two officers caught M16 rounds to their face. Detective Tillman returned fire, hitting Mr. Mets in the chest, which knocked him over the banister. He landed him on his neck, which killed him instantly.

Chapter 32

Two Days Later

Tashia couldn't take it anymore. She had to express what was on her mind. She was lying at the foot of the bed in their Hampton home watching BJ count the money he pulled out his second safe. He had Moe-B bring him every dollar he had out there in the streets. She had never seen BJ like this before. He was in straight panic mode.

"Hubby, can I speak my mind without you getting mad or without us getting into a full-fledged argument?"

"Sure, Tashia. What you got to say?"

"Well," she said, sitting up on the bed as she pulled her panties out her butt. I think you should look at the situation with Vanessa being robbed with a different set of eyes."

"Tashia, what the fuck you talking about?" BJ asked her, still counting his money.

She got off the bed and stood her sexy chocolate, Buffie Da Body in front of him. "Listen to me, BJ. Shit is serious," Tashia stated sternly. BJ stopped counting the money. "What didn't you see when we got to Vanessa's house after she called you about being rob?" BJ thought for a minute.

"Nothing," BJ replied.

"That's what I'm talking about, BJ. There was nothing. Any nigga that I know that goes into a house to rob someone that is selling drugs will ransack the whole fucking house looking for drugs and money," Tashia stated, making sense to BJ. "Whoever she claimed that came in that house, took her straight to the safe, smacked her twice then bounced with the money. They did all that barefaced, BJ." He was starting to see the picture Tashia was painting. "Not only that, but Vanessa said Toflon was the one that robbed her. We both know if he killed your mother, he would have no problem killing your sister. Instead, he left her alive. That doesn't set well with me, BJ."

BJ didn't want to think his sister did some grimy shit such as stealing his money, but she was mad about him having 40 killed. And on top of that after the robbery, Vanessa ran straight to her lover," Tashia said, looking into BJ's eyes to see if he was understood where she was going with all of this.

"Lover?" BJ said, balling his face up.

"Hell yea, boy. Ray Charles can see Moocha is sucking on Vanessa's pussy. And speaking of Moocha, she got her hands in this shit. I can bet my life on it," she told him, picking up a stack of money and helping count it.

"Damn, I missed a lot. I'm going to have to look into this," BJ said, wrapping a rubber band around a stack of money.

"Well, you need to hurry up before they spend all your damn money, buying vibrators, strap-on's and shit," Tashia said with a smirk on her face.

***

"Kay-Kay, where you get this bomb ass bud from? This shit got me high as shit," Lit Bit said, passing her best friend the blunt.

"Girl, you know my man Moe-B keep me with that good bud and that good dick."

"Bitch, whatever. That's too much information for a bitch to know," Lil Bit replied, frowning. "But when you going to tell Moe-B to hook me up with one of his friends? BJ would do just fine," she said with lustful eyes.

"Hell naw. You know he's wifeying Tashia and you know from the streets, that's one treacherous bitch. Plus, she would beat me and your ass."

"So," Lil Bit countered.

"Hell no!" Kay-Kay said jokingly but was very serious.

"Damn, bitch. You all scared and shit. But anyway, what about his other friends?" Lit Bit inquired.

"To be honest, I don't see him around too many people," Kay-Kay stated.

On the down low, Lil Bit was jealous of Kay-Kay and Moe-B's relationship. She didn't understand what Kay-Kay's chubby ass had over her. She was much smaller than her and her ass was much fatter. She felt she was definitely prettier than Kay-Kay, so she couldn't see what she had over her. *She must be letting Moe-B fuck her in the butt*, Lit Bit thought to herself.

"It's all good, girl but if he mentions that he has a friend, promise me I'll be the first person's name you mention to him."

"Lil Bit, you know I got you," Kay-Kay replied. "And who the fuck is that hugged all up with your mother? Let me find out that mom dukes is getting her freak on."

"Ummm! More like getting her smoke on!" Lil Bit said with disgust on her face.

"What? Smoke what?" Kay-Kay asked, looking confused.

"Crack! That bitch done relapsed. Ever since she been fucking with that Homicide Jack, she been smoking a hundred miles going north."

Damn, that is Homicide Jack, Kay-Kay thought to herself. He'd lost weight since the last time I saw him.

"All they getting ready to do is go in there and smoke some coke and fuck, then smoke some more. Shit, to be honest, if shit gets any worse with her, I'm going to have to ask you if I can I stay with you for a minute. You know I can't have my son around that shit too much longer," Lil Bit said, complaining.

"Lil Bit, you know you and your son are welcomed in my house. Matter of fact, let's go get his little ass now," Kay-Kay said, getting off the building stoop. They walked towards Lil Bit's mother building in Stuart Gardens better known as The G. As soon as they walked into the apartment, you could hear the moans and groans coming from her mother's room. You could hear Ronnie's headboard smacking against the wall.

Boop! Boop! Boop!

Damn. Homicide Jack have must came straight in here and jumped dead in Ronnie's pussy, Kay-Kay thought.

"Girl, you hear their trifling asses? She probably ain't even checked to see if Marcus was in the other room." Lil Bit shook her head and went to get her son out the bedroom where she found him playing his video game.

Kay-Kay tiptoed to the backdoor and unlocked it. She then pulled her phone out and called Moe-B.

"What up, Kay-Kay?" Moe-B said, answering the phone.

"Moe-B, I need you to come around The G ASAP!"

"Kay-Kay, are you good. Is everything alright?" he asked her concern.

"Yeah, baby. I'm good. I just need you around here ASAP. It's about your uncle."

"What about him?" Moe-B asked.

"I can't explain now, but I can show you though. I'm going to be in front of the building down the street in front of my girl Keashia's building. You'll see me standing out there with Lil Bit and her son."

"A'ight, I'm on my way," he agreed, ending the call.

Twenty minutes later, Moe-B walked up on Kay-Kay and Lil Bit. Marcus was riding his bike up and down the sidewalk. "What the fuck—" Kay-Kay silenced him with a kiss. He was about to get mad, but she pulled him away from Lil Bit. "Kay-Kay what's your problem?" he asked, looking around the projects for any signs of trouble.

"Listen to me!" Kay-Kay said in a whisper with her back turned to Lil Bit. She knew her friend was watching her every move. "Your uncle is a crack head," Kay-Kay said.

"Get the fuck out my face with that stupid ass shit you talking," Moe-B replied angrily, thinking she had summons him over to The G on some dumb shit.

"Moe-B, this me talking to you. You should know I don't play no type of games with you," she said with sincerity in her voice. "Your uncle is down there getting high with Lil Bit's mother right now. I left the back door unlocked so you can catch his ass in the act," Kay-Kay said, holding the front of Moe-B's shirt to stop him from walking away from her. Right on que, he looked over Kay-Kay's shoulder and saw Ronnie leaving the apartment.

"That's Lil Bit's mother right there, ain't it?" Moe-B asked.

"Yup, she must be going down to the corner store," Kay-Kay replied, looking over her shoulder.

Moe B kissed Kay-Kay on her lips and pulled away from her, going in the opposite way form Ronnie's apartment. Lil Bit rolled her eyes once she saw Moe-B kiss her friend.

"Girl, what he wanted?" Lil Bit asked her.

"Girl, you know how niggas be checking up on a bitch," Kay-Kay stated nonchalantly.

Moe-B cut through the back part of The G until he came to Lil Bit mother's back door. He looked around to see if anyone was aware of his presence. Everything looked good, so he turned the knob on the back door and entered the apartment.

The back door led into the kitchen. It was small but it was clean. The only thing that was out of place was a steak knife left out on the kitchen table. Moe-B picked the knife up and put it in his back pocket. He eased into the living room and saw it was empty. The only place left to check was the bedroom that was located down the hall.

He knew the layout of the apartment as he'd been over here a few times with Kay-Kay. He crept down the hallway. The first room on the left belonged to her mother. What he saw made him choke in rage.

There sitting on the edge of the bed, butt naked was Homicide Jack. He had a glass pipe in his mouth with a green Bic lighter at the end of the stem. The flame of the lighter was turned up high, engulfing the end of the stem. Homicide Jack looked like Pookie on *New Jack City* when he was getting high.

He pulled the .357 off his hip and walked into the room on his hero. Homicide Jack was so preoccupied with getting high that he didn't notice Moe-B entering the room until the cold steal touched his temple.

Homicide Jack killed the flames on the lighter, holding the deadly smoke in his lungs. The gun trembled just like it did that night before he killed his cousin Lil Tate. "All them years, I looked up to you. I worshipped the ground you walked on and you turned out to be a fucking crack head. I killed my own fucking cousin for a fucking glass, dick-sucking crack head who ordered me to," Moe-B said, raising his voice. "You even killed your own sister, you nephew's mother." Homicide Jack still held the smoke in his lungs. "You killed my aunt!" Moe-B pushed the gun deeper into the skin of Homicide's head. He finally let the smoke out his lungs.

"You should have never left me with them three ounces, nephew," Homicide Jack said with glazed over eyes. "It was your fault, your mistake."

Moe-B remembered he had Kay-Kay give Homicide the work and guns when he went to jail. He remembered when he went to go pick the work up, there was only two ounces in the bag.

"Bitch, this has nothing to do with me." Moe-B hauled off and slapped Homicide with the gun across his chin, knocking him out cold. Moe-B removed the knife from his back pocket and went to work.

Chapter 33

"What the fuck happened the other day, Thomas?" Detective Tillman asked his partner.

"Shit, Tillman. I'm still trying to figure it out," Detective Thomas stated, letting out a sigh of frustration. I had Internal Affairs up my ass all morning."

"You know them fuckers act as if we went into that residence with the intent to kill two elderly people," Detective Tillman said, turning off Jefferson Avenue, heading towards Stuart Gardens. "How the hell would we know that Chuck Mets was suffering from PTSD from being in the Vietnam War?" he said, shaking his head.

"And to top everything else off, we still have located Toflon. The past few days have been hectic," Detective Thomas stated, rolling his window down and spitting out of it. Detective Tillman made a right into Stuart Gardens. There was a small crowd standing behind the yellow crime scene tape.

"What the hell you think we got here?" Detective Thomas inquired.

"Uh, I don't know. The Lieutenant just assigned us this case. He told me to get over here. So here we are," Detective Tillman said, putting the car in park and getting out along with his partner.

They both ducked under the yellow crime scene tape and headed over to the cop that was standing on the porch talking with another gentleman.

"Hello, officers," Detective Tillman said, interrupting the officer'' conversation.

"Hey, detective. We've been waiting on you," the white officer said.

"What we got?" Detective Thomas asked.

"One black male dead in the first bedroom on the left. We have a witness, a Ronnie Rich who claims when she left the deceased, he was alive. She claims that she went to the store for cigarettes and beer. When she came back, the deceased was dead," the officer explained, shrugging his shoulders.

Detective Tillman and Detective Thomas made their way into the apartment. The living room was nice and clean. They could see black powder residue in the living room from the crime scene investigators dusting for prints. He slipped on a pair of latex gloves. Detective Thomas followed his partner's lead, making their way down the hall. They entered the bedroom on the left where crime scene investigators were snapping away with their cameras.

"Any identification on the deceased?" Detective Tillman asked as he walked in the room.

"No, not really, but the lady who found the body said his name was Homicide Jack. That's a helluva name right there, especially dealing with the current situation," the crime scene tech stated with a chuckle.

"I covered him up. It was kind of spooky looking at him," he told them, then resumed taking pictures.

"I'll be damned. Somebody finally caught up with Hermon 'Homicide Jack' Sparks," Detective Tillman said, pulling the sheet back. What was under the sheet both detectives were not ready for. Homicide Jack laid there eyeless with his throat slashed from ear to ear.

"Fuck! Someone worked him over good. What's that in his mouth?" Detective Thomas asked, bending down to get a closer look. He took a latex covered finger and push down on Homicide Jack's chin. Both eyeballs stared back at him. "Oh shit!" he shouted, jumping two feet back from the mutilated body. His stomach started to do flips.

"You alright?" Detective Tillman asked his partner. Detective Thomas nodded his head up and down.

"Shit, you want to see something strange?" the crime scene investigator asked, pointing to the backside of Homicide Jack. Both detectives walked around the other side of the bed and looked at what the crime tech was directing their attention to.

A glass crack pipe was hanging out of Homicide Jack's ass. Inside the pipe, held two large twenty crack rocks.

Chapter 34

"Come on, bitch! Go all the way down on the dick," Bear said, grabbing the back of Penny's head as he tried to ram his dick to the back of her throat. Penny came off his manhood spilling saliva everywhere and with an attitude.

"I'm trying to. Damn, my mouth is only but so big and your dick is way too big for my mouth," Penny said, stroking Bear's ego. The truth was Bear wasn't too good with his hygiene. He smelled just like his name and on top of that, Bear wasn't all that big in the dick department. Rose broke out in laughter.

"Girl, let me try!" Rose said, getting out the chair butt naked with her fingers dripping wet from playing in her love garden as she watched the show Bear and Penny had gave her. She could smell Bear from where she was sitting, so she knew why her girl was having trouble performing at her best.

Rose walked over and grabbed a couple of wet wipes from her Gucci handbag. She then came over to clean Bear's tiny member and peanut-sized nuts. Bear laid back on the bed like he was a king having his royal jewels cleaned. He watched Rose intensely. He'd been waiting to fuck her ever since he saw her walk to his truck with that bowlegged walk and her fat pussy print.

Bear had viewed Penny as a lady, but once she called him for a threesome and with her policy of pay to play, he looked at her in a different light. Rose grabbed a hold of Bear's member and slowly stroked him. She wondered how a nigga could be so big body wise, but had such a small dick. She smiled at her thoughts, popping Bear in her wet warm mouth like a piece of candy.

Penny was in her feelings because Rose had some wet wipes in her handbag. She didn't tell her, allowing her to suck Bear's dirty ass dick. Rose rotated her silky-smooth tongue around the head of Bear's dick.

"Sssssss," Bear moaned out, letting Rose know she was working her magic. Rose pulled him out of her mouth, spitting on his dick like a porn star then popping it back in her mouth. This seemed to get him hyped. He grabbed the back of Rose's head and started pumping into her face.

"Yeah, that's it right there. Bitch, suck this dick like a porn star," Bear said. Rose bobbed her head with every thrust that he gave her face. Penny didn't want to be left out the action, so she straddled his face.as he welcomed her glistening love box.

Penny had some pretty pussy lips and Bear was dying to suck on them. He tongue kissed her pussy on contact, leaving her no choice but to scream out one word, "Fuck!" That was Penny and Rose's signal to let each other know that their trick had some good head. Bear flicked his tongue in and out of Penny, lapping up her sweet juices. She worked her hips in a circular motion on his tongue.

"Oh shit. Oh shit, Bear. Baby, you gonna make me cum," Penny moaned out. This made him speed his tongue game up. "I'm cumming," Penny said in between breaths and jerking motions. She released in his mouth. Bear sucked her dry, leaving her with a shaky body.

"Girl, let me have some of that dick," Penny said to Rose who popped Bear's dick out of her mouth. Rose took the place of Penny on Bears' face and he didn't complain one bit. Penny eased down on Bear's dick reverse cowgirl position. She slowly worked her hips on his manhood just like she did on his tongue. She could tell that he wasn't used to good pussy. Every time she started to get into a good, steady rhythm, he would reach down and hold her still until he could get his composure together to continue.

"Oh shit! That's my song!" Penny said, jumping off Bear's now saturated dick as she went to turn the radio up that was on the hotel's dresser. The song, "Man Down" by Rihanna was playing. Penny snapped her fingers and sung along with Rihanna. She danced and made her way to the door and unlocked it, shaking the cheap hotel curtains. Bear was too engulfed in eating Rose's insides out that he wasn't paying attention to Penny movements. She went back to bouncing on Bear's tiny love stick like it was the biggest dick in the world. "Oh yeah! Give it to me, Big Daddy Bear," Penny moaned.

"Yes! Yes! Yes! Oh Bear, eat all this pussy. Eat all over it," Rose coached him, enjoying all of his tongue techniques.

A draft hit the room that alerted Bear that something was wrong. He reached under the pillow next to him for his 44 Mag, but came up empty. Bear pushed Rose off his face only to find her holding his gun with Fever and Toflon standing in the room wearing insidious grins. Penny jumped off Bear's now limp dick, rushing towards and Fever and Toflon. Rose handed Toflon Bear's gun.

"See, Bear. You are not the only one that can play the double cross game," Fever said with a smirk.

"Double cross? What are you talking about, Fever?" Bear asked.

"Aymir is what I'm talking about," Fever replied. Fever dropped the bag he was carrying and removed some rope. He gave it to Penny and Rose to tie him up. When they were done, he tied him spread eagle to the bed. Bear laid there as if he was some type of sacrifice for a shady tonic ritual.

"Come on, Fever. You go me fucked up. I've been with you since day one. You think I would betray you like that?" Bear questioned.

Fever removed two irons from his bag. "It's always the ones that closest to you," Fever replied. It was you that alerted Aymir's men to my whereabouts in the projects."

"Naw! Hell no! Fever, listen to what you are saying, fam," Bear said as he struggled to get free of the ropes.

"Naw, my fucking ass! It was you! Explain this to me. Who in the midst of a gun battle that's in their right mind, would stop and make a fucking call?"

"Man, I don't know what the fuck you are talking about. I dropped one of them muthafuckas in the projects too," Bear said, pleading his case.

"Yeah, we call that necessaries of war. Some call it casualties of war," Fever said, placing the two irons on top of Bear's man boobs, plugging them into the sockets next to the bed. "So, tell me this? You went to Aymir Jeweler's store, right?" Fever asked. Bear's eyes shot to Penny.

"You fucking bitch!" Bear could feel the irons start to heat up. He started to panic. "Come on, fam. Don't do this shit to me! Come on, Fever. Agghhhh! Agghhh!" The irons started to burn Bear's chest. Rose and Penny covered their noses trying to block out the stench of burning flesh.

"Penny, Rose. Put your clothes on and get the fuck outta here. Remember where you were supposed to dump the truck? Your car is already there waiting on you," Toflon advised them, handing them both ten thousand dollars apiece.

They jumped in their clothes, lightning speed. Rose grabbed Bear's keys off the small, round table. Then her and Penny hit the door. Toflon sat down in one of the hotel's chairs, crossing one leg over his knee like a businessman. He put some heat to the blunt that lied in the ashtray, watching Fever work.

Bear was covered in sweat as he bucked hard, trying to get the irons to roll off his chest. His skin stuck to the hot irons, keeping them in place. Fever snatched them off his chest with so much force, he pulled the scorched skin and meat with it.

"Aggggghhhh! Aggggghhhh! "Bear yelled out. Fever paid no attention to his cries. He scrapped the dead, sizzling skin off the irons with a scrapping blade. He took one of the irons and placed it on Bear's stomach, pressing down hard on it. The iron gave off a hissing sound against his stomach, sending him into a rage. "Aggghhh! Aggghhhh! Agghhhh!" Bear jerked hard, almost snapping the rope that held him in place.

Fever removed the iron, leaving a perfect iron print on Bear's stomach. Fever dugged in his bag and removed a spray bottle filled with green rubbing alcohol. He gave Bear a wicked grin before spraying his stomach and chest burns with the green alcohol. He could see tears and snot from Bear's nose from the pain he was experiencing.

"Grrrrrr! Agghhhhh! Grrrrrr!" Bear roared out, trying to fight through the excruciating pain. "I—I'm sorry, Fever. I'm sorry, fam." Bear broke down in tears.

"I know that you are. Hush, I know you are," Fever replied, kneeling down next to Bear's face.

***

"Girl, we came up tonight!" Penny yelled out, smiling ear-to-ear and fanning her face with the money Toflon had given her.

"I know. Girl, I thought for a minute we weren't going to make it up out that bitch, though," Rose stated, guiding Bear's truck though the Norfolk tunnel.

"Why you say that?" Penny asked, looking confused. "All they're going to do is rob Bear's fat ass."

"Penny, they're going to do more than that. They're going to rob and kill Bear. Why you think they paid us ten thousand each? This money is hush money, so when you get back around the way, don't be running you damn mouth," Rose said, seriously checking her running-water mouth friend.

"Bitch, I know how to keep my mouth close!" Penny said, rolling her eyes. "I like this truck though. I could see me riding around in something like this," Penny said, changing the subject.

"Yeah, this Dodge Durango isn't bad," Rose agreed, turning down a side street that led them to an abandoned factory. She smiled hard when she saw her Honda sitting behind the old factory. She parked the truck next to her car. Then she saw something odd, a parked car on the other side of the lot with no one in it.

Rose decided to pay it no mind. She and Penny got out and started to wipe down the truck, leaving no fingerprints behind. "Okay, shit looks good. Let's get our assess home."

"Shit, you ain't said nothing," Penny replied, heading to Rose's waiting Honda.

Both ladies got into the car in their own thoughts. Rose fished her car keys out of her Gucci bag and placed them in them in the ignition. She turned the key and it did nothing. "What the fuck!" she said with her face balled up.

Phuff!

The left side of Penny's face exploded. Before Rose could even figure out what had happened, her lights went out with a shot to the back of the head from. LJ silenced gun.

"Dumb ass bitches. You didn't really think Toflon was going to let you live," LJ said to himself as he reached in the back seat, retrieving both of their handbags and payment Toflon had issued them.

***

Bear was about out of it. He was on the verge of going into shock. Fever was satisfied that he obtained all the information he needed from Bear who now had trouble breathing. Fever had burnt his eyes and closed his nose. Toflon knew without a doubt that Fever was a true sadist. His phone rang. He answered on the second ring, but he didn't say anything. He just listened, then disconnected the call.

"If it brings you any comfort, Bear. Your girls Rose and Penny will meet you in hell," Fever told him with a grin in as he grabbed his 45 off his hip. He sent a shot to Bear's head, putting into a forever sleep.

Boom!

Chapter 35

BJ was in dismay when the news reached him that Homicide Jack had been brutally murdered. He knew it couldn't have been anyone but Toflon behind the murder. Channtel was calling every hour on the hour asking if had he found the people that killed her man. BJ wondered how in the hell his life became so complicated over a short period of time.

He lost his closest childhood friend Lil Chris, his mom was killed after she decided to get her life together after battling a life of addiction, his sister Vanessa hated him and now Homicide Jack was dead.

Damn, they say the streets clap back, but they never told me that they clap back hard like this, BJ thought to himself. He placed the last bullet into the AR-15 clip and slammed the clip into the assault rifle before resting it across his lap. BJ then grabbed the new Jesus piece up off the seat next to him. He went to Aymir and collected the money that he had out on Fever's head.

While we they were there, Aymir had it waiting for him. Once all this shit was over with, BJ was going to present it to Vanessa. He rubbed his fingers over the Jesus piece and whispered, "God forgive me." BJ had gotten all the information he needed to make the hit on Fever and Toflon, planning to end it all that night.

Tashia came downstairs wearing an all-black in a Gucci sweat suit and black Timberlands. She was dressed in her war gear. She looked at BJ and didn't say a word, heading straight out the door to handle her business.

***

"Tillman, what's your handle on the Homicide Jack's murder?" Detective Thomas asked his partner, while selecting a glazed doughnut out the Crispy Creme box.

"Hell, your guess is just as good as mines," he replied, pouring himself some coffee. Detective Thomas looked at his partner like he was crazy.

"You're going to drink the break room coffee?" Thomas asked.

"Shit, maybe it will bring me some much-needed luck," Detective Tillman replied with a hint of sarcasm.

Just then, the pretty fingerprint tech Ms. Bullock entered the break room. "Tillman, I've been looking for you everywhere. I see you don't know how to use your phone either." Ms. Bullock was referring to him never calling her on his off days like she had asked him to.

"I'm sorry, Bullock. But what you have for me?"

"Nope, not that easy. I want a steak dinner under candle light with me and you," she said, batting her eyes. Detective Tillman hated dating on the job because in made things difficult. He knew she had a thing for him. He figured if she left the comforts of her laptop to come down to the break room to find him and demand a dinner date, she had something serious.

"Okay, dinner date for two under candle light," he agreed. She blushed hard.

"Ok, this is what I got. I lifted the fingerprints off Bryant Jones's signed confession and I ran them in the database, getting a hit. Last year, there was a double homicide home invasion, two robbers entering the home of Jermaine Storm A.K.A. Skalez. They forced him to open his safe. Somehow Skalez got the jump on the robbers, grabs a gun and kills one of them, but the second robber kills Skalez." Ms. Bullock was talking so fast with excitement. "The deceased robber was Christian Young, a close friend of Bryant Jones."

"Ok, but what does that have to do with Bryant Jones?" Detective Thomas asked, getting impatient with her.

"There was one print on the safe and it was a positive match to Bryant Jones's print taken from the note pad he wrote his confession on," she said with a smile on her face.

Detectives Tillman and Thomas couldn't believe their luck.

"Oh, that's not all. I did some digging. Remember, the shooting that happened on twenty-fourth street a few months back? Well, one of the victims was a guy named Lil Tate. He worked for Bryant Jones and the guy they found yesterday with the glass pipe stuck in his ass. That's Homicide Jack, the enforcer for Bryant Jones. It seems like everyone around Mr. Jones is dying," Ms. Bullock said, smiling. "Now, dinner on Saturday. Pick me up at eight and don't be late. And please know that I'm not bringing my gun or panties," she stated seductively, standing on her tippy toes as she gave Detective Tillman a kiss on his cheek. Ms. Bullock left the break room floating.

Detective Thomas snatched Detective Tillman's cup of coffee out his hands and took a long sip.

"What are you doing, Thomas?" he asked him, looking confused.

"Shit, if break room coffee makes you that lucky, then shit, I need some luck too."

Chapter 36

The driver of the black Dodge Magnum watched Tashia come out her house dressed in all black looking like a thugged out Buffie da Body. He watched how her ass cheeks bounced and shook in convulsion with every step she took towards her Benz truck. The Dodge Magnum driver gritted his teeth in pure hate as he watched her back the SUV out of the driveway. He turned his ignition on, bringing his Hemi's engine to life and followed her.

***

Moocha stretched her body in the downward dog yoga position. She breathed in deeply and exhaled just the same. Normally, her 45-minute yoga session came with ease, but not today. Her mind was clouded with many things. Her brother Lance's death weighed heavily on her heart and the fact that she was in love with Vanessa, the sister of the man that killed him.

Mocha bent her body into another position and took another deep breath. Sweat dripped down her face as she concentrated hard to block the current situation out of her mind. She missed her brother Lance deeply. When her husband and daughter were murdered, Lance became her rock and her crutch. If it wasn't for him, she didn't know how she would have ever overcome the sudden death of her family.

Moocha called the only person she knew that cared for her after her family died in a home invasion. She called Lance and he took control like the big brother he was. He paid for the funeral and had Moocha move down from Harlem to Newport News, Virginia where she decided to attend nursing school.

Moocha's life started to come together with transition from Harlem to Newport News. Then all of sudden, Lance was robbed and murdered. It was deja vu all over again. Moocha took another deep breath and closed her eyes. She still could hear the last conversation she had with Lance.

"What's up, sis?" Lance said once he heard Moocha on the other end of the phone.

"Big Bruh! You know it works with me. This hospital got me working a double shift tonight, but I'm not complaining though," she replied in a happy voice.

"Well, that's good you're staying busy and stacking that paper at the same time. I really want you to know I'm proud of you and admire your strength," he told her with sincerity in his voice.

"Bruh, you got me smiling over here," Moocha said, smiling through the phone. "Bruh, can I ask you something?"

"Yeah? What's up?"

"When are you going to get out the streets and settle down and get married?" she asked.

"Sis, to be honest, I'm working on it. I've been having those same thoughts lately. I have made my mark in the game, so it's about time I make my exit. Plus, I met this great woman that got me thinking she is the one," Lance confessed.

"What? My brother found someone that can tame his pussy hungry ass?" Moocha replied with excitement in her voice.

"Yup, and she'd a straight cutie, too. She got a big ole butt to match some big ole brea—"

"Aye, I don't need to know all that. When can I meet her?" Moocha asked, cutting her brother off. Lance started laughing.

"My bad, sis. Well, we're going on a boat ride tonight. So, I guess I'm set something up for you to meet her the day after tomorrow," Lance stated.

"Damn, she must be something special if she got your ass taking boat rides and shit," she teased, laughing. "At least tell me the girl's name?"

"Oh, it's Tashia."

The knock on the door snapped her out of her thoughts. She broke her yoga pose and answered the door. She was expecting someone, but surprised to see Tashia standing on the other side of her door. "Hi, Tashia," she said, greeting her with a fake smile on her face. She knew Tashia didn't care too much for her.

"What's up, Moocha?" Tashia replied with an evenly bogus smile on her face.

"How are you doing? Is Vanessa here?" she asked.

"No, she stepped out for a few to run some errands." Moocha wiped sweat from her forehead. "But you are welcomed to sit and wait for her if you like. She shouldn't be much longer," Moocha said, opening the apartment door wider to let her in. Since she was aware Tashia disliked her, she knew came there for a reason.

"Okay. Yeah, I'll wait for her. How long has she been gone?" Tashia asked her as she stepped into their love nest.

"She's been gone about a hour," Moocha replied, closing the door behind her.

From what Tashia could see, Moocha's living conditions weren't bad. The peanut butter colored leather sectional sofa was perfect on top of the tan carpet. The whole living room was coordinated from the curtains to the wall color. The peanut butter and tan color had set a relaxing tone throughout the apartment.

Tashia sat on the sofa, placing her Chanel bag on the brown coffee table that was in front of the sofa. "Would you like anything to drink?" Moocha asked her.

"Naw, I'm good. I got a bottle of water in my bag."

"Okay, well as you can see, I'm sweaty from yoga. I'm going to take me a quick shower and freshen up. If you want, you can watch some T.V." Moocha then slid the remote to her that controlled the 60-inch television.

"Thanks!" Tashia said with a smile, grabbing the remote. Moocha headed to the bathroom. Tashia rolled her eyes at her back and wrinkled her nose up at Moocha's yoga pants that were deeply embedded in between the crack of her ass.

"Stank ass bitch," she mumbled under her breath. She couldn't wait for Moocha to enter the bathroom and hear the water running in the shower.

She quickly started searching her apartment for any sign of the money she suspected they stole from BJ. She crept past the bathroom. She could hear Moocha in the shower humming a tune. She entered a room on the right. Everything was laid out nice and neat in the room. The king-sized bed was made and the air in the room smelled fresh.

Tashia quickly looked under the bed and in between the mattress. She went to the small closet and checked the shelf, pushing the clothes to the side that hung on the hangers and searching the back of the closet. She came up short.

Then she exited the room and made her way down the hall to the second bedroom. She could still hear the shower running. She wasted no time when she entered the bedroom. She figured this must be the room they sleep in as the bed was unmade. Tashia repeated the same search she did in the first room. Still, she found nothing.

She opened a drawer on the nightstand next to the bed and found about six different dildos that were different shapes and sizes. Tashia went to the closet and saw a gym bag lying there in plain sight. She bent down and opened the bag. Instantly, she became angry. "I knew that these bitches stole that money," she said to herself as she stared at the stack of bills that rested in the bag. She zipped the bag back up and was ready to leave when a picture on the wall caught her attention.

She went over to the picture that sat on the nightstand where the dildos were. She sat the bag down near her feet, picking up the framed picture.

Tashia's mouth dropped open. The photo was of Moocha and Lance at some club she didn't recognize. Tashia pulled the picture out of the frame and flipped it over to the back. It read:

We party like true bosses! 2008 New Years.
Love you, sis

She flipped the photo back to the front and examined it one last time before placing it back inside the frame. She then placed it back on the nightstand.

"Damn. Nigga, you just won't die. We killed your ass over a year ago and your fat ass still resurfaced somehow," Tashia to herself. She picked up the bag up and turned around only to find standing there, Moocha holding a 38 snub she got out BJ's safe. Tashia froze.

Moocha mumbled, "This is for Lance, bitch." She pulled the trigger, sending a lone shot through Tashia's right eye.

Bong!

Chapter 37

Vanessa pulled up to Moocha's apartment complex. She got out of the car and headed to the truck to remove the items she purchased from the grocery shopping. She wanted to show Moocha she could pull she own weight. Especially since she'd been catering to her ever since she'd gotten out the hospital.

Vanessa had fallen in love with Moocha, but she still wasn't sure if she was gay or not. She still had a craving for some good hard dick. The strap ons and the dildos were awesome, but they could never compare to a real dick.

Vanessa struggled to carry a heavy bag. She didn't want to call Moocha for help. She wanted to at least get the bags to the front door of the apartment before she asked for help. She hadn't regained her full strength back after being shot and all the surgeries she had been through.

Shit, these two gallons of milk are heavy like two cinderblocks, Vanessa thought as she carried the first bag to the door of the apartment. She sat the bag down and went back to the car to retrieve the others.

She was already winded, building up a small sweat. She grabbed the last of the four bags that sat at the back of the car. She took two steps and stumbled a little until a hand steadied her.

"Take your time, Vanessa," a voice said behind her.

She looked back and smiled at Wallo. "Hey, Wallo. Thank you," she said, pleased she was saved from the embarrassment of falling in public.

"Ain't no problem. Here, let me help you," Wallo offered, taking the bags from Vanessa's hands. He slowly walked with her to the front door of her apartment.

"Where are you coming from?" she asked him. "I didn't know that you be around Chestnut Avenue."

"You know how a nigga be. I'm always breezing through Bad News somewhere," Wallo said, stopping at Vanessa's door. She stood in front of Wallo and her eyes started to water.

His head was on swirl. He lost Tashia's whereabouts. He knew she was in the apartment complex because he saw her Benz truck in the parking lot, but he also saw that Vanessa was hurting.

"I miss him every day, Wallo. I miss Rob— I mean 40. I miss every damn day," she cried.

"I miss him too, Vanessa," he admitted, putting the bags down and embracing her. "I'm gonna make whoever did this pay," he whispered in her ear as he held her.

Bong!

The gunshot made them both jump. They heard the shot coming from the other side of the door.

"Moocha!" Vanessa fumbled with her keys, trying to get them into the lock. Opening the door, Vanessa rushed into the apartment with Wallo on her heels.

"Moocha! Moocha!" she called out, heading back towards the bedrooms after she found the living room empty. Moocha didn't respond. The first bedroom was empty. Vanessa made her way to the master bedroom. Her heart was pumping harder than a nigga fresh out of prison, getting his first piece of pussy. When she walked through the threshold of the master bedroom, she stopped in her tracks, her knees buckling. She caught herself on the doorframe of the bedroom, trying to stop herself from falling.

There was Tashia lying dead on the floor with an eye missing and the bedroom smelling of gunpowder and death. The nerves in her body were still alive as her left leg twitched and jerked. Moocha stood over Tashia still holding the 38 snub. Wallo eased up beside Moocha, slowly removing the gun out her hands.

When he did, she snapped out her trance. An imperceptible amount of relief from her brother's murder came over her. She looked at Wallo as he wasn't from this planet.

"Moocha!" Vanessa called out.

She turned and faced Vanessa who was still posted against the doorframe. She rushed towards her, embraced her.

"She found the money. I had to do something. She killed my brother Lance," Moocha cried.

Wallo couldn't believe what he had just heard. "Hold on. Do you think anyone heard the gun shot?" he asked her.

"I don't think so. Both of our neighbors are at work. There's no one in the apartment next to us," Vanessa replied.

"Who is this, Vanessa?" Moocha inquired.

"This is 40's friend."

"Do you think you can help us get rid of the body?" Moocha asked as if she was unfazed by the dead woman lying in her bedroom. She had fire in her eyes as if she been there before.

"I might but we can't do it right now. It's still daylight outside. Plus, you got to tell me more about what's going on," Wallo replied. He escorted them out the room, closing the bedroom door behind them. He used his T-shirt to touch the door knob.

They entered the living room. Moocha and Vanessa sat next to each other on the sofa while Wallo went and peeked out the window. Everything looked normal. "So, who is Lance?" Wallo asked, but already had a clue who he was.

"Lance is my brother. A year ago, my brother was robbed and murdered. Vanessa's brother and girl killed my brother. I found out from you, Vanessa. It was when you told me your brother told you about the robbery he pulled on Lance." Moocha said, looking at Vanessa and Wallo.

"Why didn't you tell me?" Vanessa asked.

"Because you didn't have nothing to do with the murder of my brother and because I'm in love with you," Moocha said with sincerity in her voice and eyes.

Vanessa reached over and touched Moocha's hand. Wallo's mind was going wild. He couldn't believe that this bitch was talking about the same murder 40 and Tashia had pulled with Block and Skalez. There was one piece missing to him. He didn't know where did BJ's role came in at.

"Vanessa, who is your brother again?" Wallo questioned.

"Umm, BJ."

"BJ that used to hang on twenty-fourth street?"

"Yeah, that's him," she replied. Wallo gripped the 38 snub in his hand.

"Ok, this is what we are going to do. Pack some clothes and grab that money you were talking about. I'm going to take you both to a hotel. Then I'm coming back to move the body tonight. But you got to help me wrap Tashia's body up first." Wallo said, stepping away from the window.

Vanessa was reluctant to touch her body but she saw Moocha didn't have a problem with it, so she went along with it. Moocha lead the way as Wallo brought up the rear.

"The money is already packed up," Moocha told him, pointing to the gym bag that was next to Tashia's body.

Moocha went and snatched the comforter off the bed to wrap her body in. Wallo grabbed the pillow off the bed, walking behind Moocha. He pushed the pillow to the back of her head and squeezed the trigger.

Bong!

The gunshot was muffled but loud enough for Vanessa to hear, spinning around in fear.

"What are you doing, Wallo?" Vanessa rushed over to her now dead lover. He stood over Vanessa clutching Moocha's in her arms.

"I'm avenging my cousin Skalez's death."

Bong!

Vanessa's head snapped forward. Wallo shot her in the top of her head, the bullet exiting her chin.

Bong! Bong!

He dropped two more shots in her. He felt a little better now that he got some get back for Skalez's murder. Wallo picked the gym bag up off the floor, exiting the apartment unheard and unseen with BJ now on his mind.

Chapter 38

BJ sat on the corner of 16th street watching Fever's crew fall into the small restaurant, The Grill. He'd been calling Moe-B all day, but he didn't get an answer. Moe-B was supposed to make the hit with him. "Bitch ass nigga didn't even show up," he said to himself. He felt like Moe-B turned bitch since his uncle got murdered. The last time he saw was the day before. He'd given him three bricks to be broken down and distributed to their workers at the trap houses.

BJ made a call, learning the work had been delivered to the trap house, so he wasn't worried he had may have ran off. He picked his phone up and dialed Moe-B's number one last time and he got the same result. He was sent to voice mail.

BJ saw a jet-black 600 Benz pull up in front of The Grill. "That must be him," he spoke out loud to himself, going off the information Aymir provided him. Toflon pulled up right behind the Benz in his blue Lexus. BJ lit the blunt that rested in the ashtray.

"Fuck Moe-B," he mumbled and took a few pulls of the blunt. He reached and grabbed the AR-15 off the back seat. BJ was waiting for Fever and Toflon to get comfortable before he made his move. He inhaled the weed deeply, pulling his vest over his chest and strapping it on as he waited.

***

Fever walked in The Grill with Toflon following behind him. This was Toflon's first time at one of their get togethers, so he was leery. Fever's uncle owned the establishment. The Grill wasn't that popular but with Fever and his crew meeting there weekly, Fever made it worth the while for his uncle. Especially since he paid the rent every month for The Grill.

They stood to their feet as their boss entered The Grill. "My fucking niggas," Fever said, approaching the tables in the center of the restaurant.

"What's up, boss man!" A few crewmembers said, greeting their boss with smiles. Fever's uncle, Ben, began to bring the feast of food out and placed it on the table.

"Nephew! What's going on, youngster?" Fever's snaggled toothed Uncle Ben said with a toothless smile.

"You know, Unc. Just the same ole two step trying to stack this paper at the same time," he replied, embracing his uncle in a bear hug. "What you got for us this week, Unc?" he asked as he stepped away and stared at the food that laid out on the table.

"Well, we got fried chicken with my secret bar-b-que sauce, baked mac and cheese, greens, mashed potatoes with gravy, baby back ribs, corn bread and for desert, my wife's homemade upside-down pineapple cake."

"Damn, Unc. You getting a nigga hungry just talking about it," Fever said, licking his big lips. He took a seat. Toflon then took a seat to his right where Bear would have normally sat. An old timer then sat Fever's left. Toflon had never saw the man before, but he could sense the guy was a killer. He had that look in his eyes that only another killer could recognize. There were eight men who sat around the table with two more men posted up by the front door.

"Aye, listen up!" Fever said, drawing his crew's complete attention. "We're going to take this city over not only flooding this bitch with the best purp and sour loud this city has ever seen, but we're selling coke, too. We selling dimes, double ups, wholesales to weight. If a nigga not buying our shit and selling it, then he's not eating. Next, we're hitting the projects. I got every nigga in the projects that's making some noise and doing some figures with the coke on board."

"You see these eight right here?" Fever said, eyeing every man at the table. "We 're going to run this city with a iron fist. I will call a meeting at the end of the week to provide more details. But for now, I got some news for you all." Fever paused. "As you can see, Bear is not sitting amongst us anymore." Fever paused again, looking into the eyes of his most loyal soldiers.

"Bear decided to commit treason in the worse way. When someone tried to kill me in Riley Circle projects, well that was Bear's work of treason." A few soldiers mumbled under their breath. "It's all good though because Bear got his issues," Fever said, leaving his soldiers to form their own opinions as to what happened to Bear. "As for now, this is the new muscle for the crew," Fever said, pointing to Toflon. Some of the men around the table nodded their heads up and down in agreement. Many of them heard about Toflon's gun game. "And here is LJ. He is the quiet muscle behind the muscle, if you know what I mean," Fever said with a grin. "Duck, you got that?" Fever asked.

Duck passed a folded piece of white paper to him across the table from where he sat. Fever handed the paper to Toflon. "I told you I would let you handle the kid BJ, so here you go."

Toflon unfolded the piece of paper. It had an address scribbled on it. "My man Duck ran into a dude named Moe-B and BJ's name came up. He turned over the address with no problem. I even had Duck go by there to see if it was official and everything checked out. BJ stays there with his girl Tashia." Toflon jumped up from his chair. Fever put a hand on his arm, stopping him. "Can this wait until after dinner?" Fever asked him.

Toflon looked at him crazy. "Naw, this is for Butta!"

Fever nodded his head up and down in agreement and whispered, "Give him two to the head for me." Toflon turned on his heels and walked out The Grill to go kill BJ.

***

BJ waited long enough. He started the car, driving to the alley was behind The Grill. Everything was just like Bear described to Aymir. BJ could see an old man moving back and forth in the kitchen through the opened back door. BJ slid two extra clips in his back pockets and checked the AR-15 to make sure one was in the chamber.

He pulled the hood of his hoodie over his head and pulled the Jesus piece out, letting it hang down on his chest. He made his way to the opened back door of The Grill. The alley was quiet and the night breeze was cool on BJ's skin. He took a deep breath and eased inside the kitchen with the assault rifle, pointing it at the back of the old man's head. "Put your hands in the air and move towards the freezer." Ben followed BJ's orders. He was scared as hell. He didn't want to die tonight.

"Listen, you don't have to do this, man. The money is in my back pocket. Just take it and leave," Ben said with a shaky old man's voice.

"Man, shut the fuck up and get in the freezer and if you make any noise I'm going to come back and kill your ass," BJ spoke through clenched teeth. Ben stepped in the freezer, then BJ closed the door behind him.

He crept out into the dinner area where Fever and his men were laughing and chowing down on Ben's good ole cooking. Duck was the first one to see BJ with the deadly weapon. He couldn't alert his friends because his mouth was stuffed with corn bread. Duck rose to his feet only to get his chest opened up with the AR-15.

Yak! Yak! Yak! Yak! Yak! Yak!

BJ came out the kitchen splitting Fever's soldiers as they scrambled to leave, taking hot bullets in the process.

Yak! Yak! Yak! Yak! Yak! Yak!

The AR-15 jumped in BJ's hand with ease. Instantly, Fever's men were all twisted, lying on the floor dead. The ones that weren't dead were breathing their last breath before they died. Fever was on the floor lying on his back with two holes in his chest. He desperately fought to get to his 45 Ruger that rested in the small of his back. With the weight of his body and the two holes in his chest, it was an impossible task for him. BJ went from man to man, searching for Toflon. Every man he found alive, he put a bullet in his head.

BJ rolled a dark-skinned dude over with his foot. He was still alive. "Where's Toflon?" he asked. The dark-skinned dude tried to respond, but he started choking on his own blood. "Tsk, tsk!" BJ sucked his teeth, putting one in the dude's face.

Yak!

BJ made his way over to Fever who struggled to breath, his lungs starting to fill with blood. "Where's Toflon?" BJ asked him, pointing the AR-15 at him. Fever chuckled at him, showing him his blood-stained teeth.

"Fuck you!" Fever said, gasping for air.

BJ knew he didn't have much time. "Listen, tough guy. This right here is from Aymir. And by the way, I heard you was looking for me. I'm BJ."

"Damn," Fever mumbled.

Yak! Yak! Yak!

BJ let off three shots, putting Fever down like a dog in the streets. BJ made a left, leaving out the way that he came. He even left Fever's uncle in the freezer so he could freeze to death.

Chapter 39

BJ was livid that Toflon had somehow escaped his wrath. Hit the blunt again as he headed towards his Hampton home. He called Moe-B three times since he hit Fever. He didn't know what was going on but his world seemed so small right now. He'd been calling Tashia and she hadn't picked up her phone either. Shit, she might be home sleep, BJ thought to himself.

Lately, she'd been distant. He knew she was upset sine he hadn't confronted Vanessa about the bogus robbery she pulled on him. He needed to figure out how he was going to get his shit back in order. He remembered a few short years ago, his friend Lil Chris told him that you couldn't have a heart out here in this game because it always got in your way when it was time to make a hard decision.

"Damn, I miss you my nigga," BJ said out loud, as he thought about Lil Chris. He took another pull from the blunt. Shit didn't feel right to him, so he kept checking his mirrors. He took the ill vibe as paranoia from murking Fever and his crew.

BJ adjusted the AR-15 that was across his lap. He turned down the street where he lived. Things looked normal but just for good measure, he drove past his house and circled the block. Coming back around, BJ pulled over and parked in front of his house instead of parking in the driveway.

He changed the clip on the assault rifle and checked his surroundings, slamming a round in the chamber of the AR-15. His mental alarm was going off. "Damn, this weed got me paranoid like a muthafucka," he said, climbing out his Charger.

He looked around and saw a brown van parked about four cars down from where he was. He had never saw the van before. He spit on the ground, making his way to his house with the AR-15 held closely to his side. He then heard running footsteps coming up from behind him. He whirled around, bringing the AR-15 up as he came face to face with Toflon who was pointing his Mack 10 at him.

They were a stand still. Toflon gritted his teeth. He should've waited until BJ came clearly from around the car. Had he done that, he would have saw him carrying the AR-15. BJ wondered how this was going to end, wishing he had listened to his instincts.

"We finally meet face to face, gun to gun," BJ said.

"So, what is it going to be, nigga? We gonna spark it out?" Toflon said, gripping the Mack 10 he pointed at him even tighter.

BJ knew there was no way he was going to let Toflon there here alive. From the looks of it, Toflon's body language suggested he had the same intentions. BJ squeezed a little tighter on the trigger of the AR-15.

"Freeze! Drop your weapons!" The brown van's lights came on and plain-clothes officers started exiting with their glocks drawn. More vehicle lights came on and so did more officers with their weapons locked, loaded and ready. "This is Newport News' Homicide branch accompanied by the Hampton Police Department. Drop your weapons! You both are wanted for murder." Detective Tillman's voice came through the loud speaker.

BJ and Toflon both stared at each other, still holding firmly to their weapons. "You heard that? Murder, huh? I heard you graduated and now you playing with them big boys now, little nigga," Toflon said, clutching his gun.

"Shit, I been playing with them big boys. That's why you was trying to get my paper from me, remember?" BJ shot back. Toflon started to chuckle.

"You know what? I like you, little nigga. But listen, any day is a good day to die. But it's never a good day to go to jail for murder," Toflon told him.

"Drop your weapons!" Detective Tillman voice came through the loud speaker again.

"Let's dead our beef for now and deal with the situation at hand," Toflon suggested, nodding his head towards the armed police.

A calmness came over BJ. He no longer felt fear in his body. BJ nodded his head up and down in agreement. It was like the both of them knew their next move. They both turned their weapons on the waiting officers and opened fire.

Yak! Yak! Yak! Yak! Yak! Yak! Yak!

BJ's AR-15 roared, bringing his quiet neighborhood to life.

Rak! Rak! Rak! Rak! Rak! Rak!

Toflon's Mack 10 banged hard in his hand, sending the detectives and officers ducking for cover and shooting blindly.

Blocka! Blocka! Blocka! Blocka! Blocka!

The police returned fire. BJ could hear bullets zipping past his head. A bullet struck Toflon in the chest and elbow, making him stumble in between two parked cars. This didn't stop him from letting off shots.

Rak! Rak! Rak!

"Aghh! Shit," BJ cried out as a bullet pierced his thigh and shoulder. He made a dash for it in between the houses.

Toflon stopped shooting, reloading the Mack 10 with a fresh clip. He checked his chest wound when he pulled his hand away. It was a dark-colored blood. He knew that wasn't a good sign. He started feeling light-headed. He struggled to get to his feet. He could see the police moving in on him, boxing him in. He sprung up, gripping the Mack 10 hard then squeezing the trigger even harder.

Rak! Rak! Rak! Rak! Rak! Rak!

The police opened fire, another bullet hitting Toflon in the chest. It knocked him back on the trunk of a parked car.

Blocka! Blocka! Blocka! Blocka! Blocka!

Toflon continued to fire not totally focusing his shots at one particular officer, but shooting wildly at them.

Rak! Rak! Rak! Rak! Rak! Rak!

The officers sent a wall of bullets Toflon's way, striking him in his face and neck. He crashed to the ground still clutching the Mack 10.

***

BJ limped hard, moving as fast as he could. The bullet burned the hell out of his leg and his shoulder. His body become numb from the wounds. "Fuck! I got to get somewhere safe and figure shit out," BJ said to himself as he kept moving between the houses.

He could hear Toflon banging it out with the police. BJ wanted to stop but he knew he had to get as far away from the police as possible. He came out between some houses three blocks over. He needed some wheels.

Headlights lit the street up as he saw a car was coming. BJ faded back in between the houses. Then the car stopped. "Yo, BJ! Come on, fam!" a voice called out from the car.

BJ wasn't familiar with the black Dodge Magnum or the driver. It was dark and he could barely see the driver from where he was hiding. He couldn't be picky in this situation. If someone wanted to help him out of a jam, then he was going to take it.

BJ ditched the AR-15 and limped towards the black Dodge Magnum. Three feet away from the car, the driver's door opened. Wallo stepped out holding a 9-millimeter Ruger. He wore a wicked grin. BJ stopped in his tracks. His hand went to the Jesus piece that hung around his neck. He held it in his hand firmly.

Wallo pointed the gun at him. He had watched whole situation unfold with BJ and the police from the top of the block. He saw him take flight between the houses, deciding to pursue him. Now here he was, staring down the sight at the man who killed his cousin.

"Skalez told me to let you hold these for him. I already gave Tashia and Vanessa theirs."

Bong! Bong! Bong!

Wallo sent three hallow points into BJ's head, dropping him instantly. Blood and brain matter oozed out of the holes from his cranium. Wallo stood over BJ's slumped body. He looked at how he laid dead on the ground still holding the Jesus piece in his hand. Chuckling, he said, "When the streets clap back, niggas always turn to God!"

He bent over and removed the Jesus piece from around BJ's neck. "Game over, bitch ass nigga!"

Wallo walked away and jumped in his Magnum. As he distanced himself from the crime scene, he looked out of the windshield up to the sky. "Rest in peace, homie," he said to Skalez.

For a brief moment, the sky seemed to light up as a star twinkled brightly. Wallo interpreted that as a sign that Skalez was smiling down on him. "Watch over me and keep me safe out here, my nigga. Much love."

He turned on some music and drove off into the night.

THE END

Submission Guideline

Submit the first three chapters of your completed manuscript to ldpsubmissions@gmail.com, subject line: Your book's title. The manuscript must be in a .doc file and sent as an attachment. Document should be in Times New Roman, double spaced and in size 12 font. Also, provide your synopsis and full contact information. If sending multiple submissions, they must each be in a separate email.

Have a story but no way to send it electronically? You can still submit to LDP/Ca$h Presents. Send in the first three chapters, written or typed, of your completed manuscript to:

LDP: Submissions Dept
Po Box 870494
Mesquite, Tx 75187

DO NOT send original manuscript. Must be a duplicate.

Provide your synopsis and a cover letter containing your full contact information.

Thanks for considering LDP and Ca$h Presents.

Coming Soon from Lock Down Publications/Ca$h Presents

BOW DOWN TO MY GANGSTA

By **Ca$h**

TORN BETWEEN TWO

By **Coffee**

BLOOD STAINS OF A SHOTTA **III**

By **Jamaica**

STEADY MOBBIN

By **Marcellus Allen**

BLOOD OF A BOSS **V**

By **Askari**

LOYAL TO THE GAME **IV**

By **T.J. & Jelissa**

A DOPEBOY'S PRAYER **II**

By **Eddie "Wolf" Lee**

IF LOVING YOU IS WRONG… **III**

LOVE ME EVEN WHEN IT HURTS

By **Jelissa**

TRUE SAVAGE **V**

By **Chris Green**

TRAPHOUSE KING **III**

By **Hood Rich**

BLAST FOR ME **III**

By **Ghost**

ADDICTIED TO THE DRAMA **III**

By **Jamila Mathis**

LIPSTICK KILLAH **III**

CRIME OF PASSION **II**

By **Mimi**

WHAT BAD BITCHES DO **III**

THE BOSS MAN'S DAUGHTERS **V**

By **Aryanna**

THE COST OF LOYALTY **II**

By **Kweli**

SHE FELL IN LOVE WITH A REAL ONE **II**

By **Tamara Butler**

LOVE SHOULDN'T HURT **II**

By **Meesha**

CORRUPTED BY A GANGSTA **III**

By **Destiny Skai**

A GANGSTER'S CODE II

By **J-Blunt**

KING OF NEW YORK II

By **T.J. Edwards**

CUM FOR ME **IV**

By **Ca$h & Company**

Available Now

RESTRAINING ORDER **I & II**

By **CA$H & Coffee**

LOVE KNOWS NO BOUNDARIES **I II & III**

By **Coffee**

RAISED AS A GOON I, II, III & IV

BRED BY THE SLUMS I, II, III

BLAST FOR ME I & II

By **Ghost**

LAY IT DOWN **I & II**

LAST OF A DYING BREED

BLOOD STAINS OF A SHOTTA I & II

By **Jamaica**

LOYAL TO THE GAME

LOYAL TO THE GAME II

LOYAL TO THE GAME III

By **TJ & Jelissa**

BLOODY COMMAS I & II

SKI MASK CARTEL I II & III

KING OF NEW YORK

By **T.J. Edwards**

IF LOVING HIM IS WRONG…I & II

By **Jelissa**

WHEN THE STREETS CLAP BACK I & II III

By **Jibril Williams**

A DISTINGUISHED THUG STOLE MY HEART I II & III

LOVE SHOULDN'T HURT

By **Meesha**

A GANGSTER'S CODE

By J-Blunt

PUSH IT TO THE LIMIT

By **Bre' Hayes**

BLOOD OF A BOSS **I, II, III & IV**

By **Askari**

THE STREETS BLEED MURDER **I, II & III**

THE HEART OF A GANGSTA I II& III

By **Jerry Jackson**

CUM FOR ME

CUM FOR ME 2

CUM FOR ME 3

An **LDP Erotica Collaboration**

BRIDE OF A HUSTLA **I II & II**

THE FETTI GIRLS **I, II& III**

CORRUPTED BY A GANGSTA I & II

By **Destiny Skai**

WHEN A GOOD GIRL GOES BAD

By **Adrienne**

A GANGSTER'S REVENGE **I II III & IV**

THE BOSS MAN'S DAUGHTERS

THE BOSS MAN'S DAUGHTERS II

THE BOSSMAN'S DAUGHTERS III

THE BOSSMAN'S DAUGHTERS IV

A SAVAGE LOVE **I & II**

BAE BELONGS TO ME

A HUSTLER'S DECEIT I, II

WHAT BAD BITCHES DO I, II

By **Aryanna**

A KINGPIN'S AMBITON

A KINGPIN'S AMBITION **II**

I MURDER FOR THE DOUGH

By **Ambitious**

TRUE SAVAGE

TRUE SAVAGE II

TRUE SAVAGE **III**

TRUE SAVAGE **IV**

By **Chris Green**

A DOPEBOY'S PRAYER

By **Eddie "Wolf" Lee**

THE KING CARTEL **I, II & III**

By **Frank Gresham**

THESE NIGGAS AIN'T LOYAL **I, II & III**

By **Nikki Tee**

GANGSTA SHYT **I II &III**

By **CATO**

THE ULTIMATE BETRAYAL

By **Phoenix**

BOSS'N UP **I , II & III**

By **Royal Nicole**

I LOVE YOU TO DEATH

By Destiny J

I RIDE FOR MY HITTA

I STILL RIDE FOR MY HITTA

By **Misty Holt**

LOVE & CHASIN' PAPER

By **Qay Crockett**

TO DIE IN VAIN

By **ASAD**

BROOKLYN HUSTLAZ

By **Boogsy Morina**

BROOKLYN ON LOCK I & II

By **Sonovia**

GANGSTA CITY

By **Teddy Duke**

A DRUG KING AND HIS DIAMOND I & II

A DOPEMAN'S RICHES

By Nicole Goosby

TRAPHOUSE KING I & II

By **Hood Rich**

LIPSTICK KILLAH **I, II**

CRIME OF PASSION

By **Mimi**

BOOKS BY LDP'S CEO, CA$H

TRUST IN NO MAN

TRUST IN NO MAN 2

TRUST IN NO MAN 3

BONDED BY BLOOD

SHORTY GOT A THUG

THUGS CRY

THUGS CRY 2

THUGS CRY 3

TRUST NO BITCH

TRUST NO BITCH 2

TRUST NO BITCH 3

TIL MY CASKET DROPS

RESTRAINING ORDER

RESTRAINING ORDER 2

IN LOVE WITH A CONVICT

Coming Soon

BONDED BY BLOOD 2

BOW DOWN TO MY GANGSTA